The Escape of the Deadly Dinosaur:
USA

The Search for the Sunken Treasure:
Australia

The Mystery of the Mona Lisa:
France

The Caper of the Crown Jewels:
England

BOOKS 1–4

Elizabeth Singer Hunt
Illustrated by Brian Williamson

WEINSTEIN
BOOKS

Printed in the United States of America.

Cataloging-in-Publication data for this book is available
from the Library of Congress.

ISBN: 978-1-60286-325-5 (print)

Published by Weinstein Books
A member of the Perseus Books Group
www.weinsteinbooks.com

Weinstein Books are available at special discounts
for bulk purchases in the U.S. by corporations,
institutions and other organizations. For more
information, please contact the
Special Markets Department at
the Perseus Books Group,
2300 Chestnut Street, Suite 200,
Philadelphia, PA 19103,
call (800) 810-4145, ext. 5000, or
e-mail special.markets@perseusbooks.com.

First edition

10 9 8 7 6 5 4 3 2 1

The Escape of the
Deadly Dinosaur:
USA

BOOK ①

Join Agent Jack Stalwart on his adventures:

The Escape of the Deadly Dinosaur: USA

Elizabeth Singer Hunt

Illustrated by Brian Williamson

WEINSTEIN
BOOKS

ISBN: 978-1-60286-004-9

First Edition
15 14 13 12

For Catherine, Darcy, Patricia, and Toni

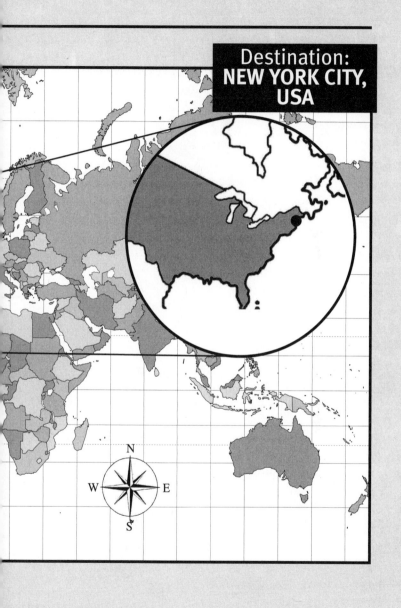
Destination:
NEW YORK CITY, USA

JACK STALWART

Jack Stalwart applied to be a secret
agent for the Global Protection
Force four months ago.

My name is Jack Stalwart. My older brother,
Max, was a secret agent for you, until he
disappeared on one of your missions. Now I
want to be a secret agent, too. If you choose
me, I will be an excellent secret agent and get
rid of evil villains, just like my brother did.
Sincerely,

Jack Stalwart

THINGS YOU'LL FIND IN EVERY BOOK

 **Watch Phone:** The only gadget Jack wears all the time, even when he's not on official business. His Watch Phone is the central gadget that makes most others work. There are lots of important features, most importantly the *C* button, which reveals the code of the day – necessary to unlock Jack's Secret Agent Book Bag. There are buttons on both sides, one of which ejects his lifesaving Melting Ink Pen. Beyond these functions, it also works as a phone and, of course, gives Jack the time of day.

 **Global Protection Force (GPF):** The GPF is the organization Jack works for. It's a worldwide force of young secret agents whose aim is to protect the world's people, places, and possessions. No one knows exactly where its main offices are located (all correspondence and gadgets for repair are sent to a special PO Box, and training is held at various locations around the world), but Jack thinks it's somewhere cold, like the Arctic Circle.

Whizzy: Jack's magical miniature globe. Almost every night at precisely 7:30 PM, the GPF uses Whizzy to send Jack the identity of the country that he must travel to. Whizzy can't talk, but he can cough up messages. Jack's parents don't know Whizzy is anything more than a normal globe.

The Magic Map: The magical map hanging on Jack's bedroom wall. Unlike most maps, the GPF's map is made of a mysterious wood. Once Jack inserts the country piece from Whizzy, the map swallows Jack whole and sends him away on his missions. When he returns, he arrives precisely one minute after he left.

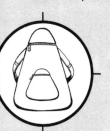

Secret Agent Book Bag: The Book Bag that Jack wears on every adventure. Licensed only to GPF secret agents, it contains top-secret gadgets necessary to foil bad guys and escape certain death. To activate the bag before each mission, Jack must punch in a secret code given to him by his Watch Phone. Once he's away, all he has to do is place his finger on the zipper, which identifies him as the owner of the bag and it immediately opens.

THE STALWART FAMILY

Jack's dad, John

He moved the family to England when Jack was two, in order to take a job with an aerospace company. As far as Jack knows, his dad designs and manufactures aeroplane parts. Jack's dad thinks he is an ordinary boy and that his other son, Max, attends a school in Switzerland. Jack's dad is American and his mum is British, which makes Jack a bit of both.

Jack's mum, Corinne

One of the greatest mums as far as Jack is concerned. When she and her husband received a letter from a posh school in Switzerland inviting Max to attend, they were overjoyed. Since Max left six months ago, they have received numerous notes in Max's handwriting telling them he's OK. Little do they know it's all a lie and that it's the GPF sending those letters.

Jack's older brother, Max

Two years ago, at the age of nine, Max joined the GPF. Max used to tell Jack about his adventures and show him how to work his secret-agent gadgets. When the family received a letter inviting Max to attend a school in Europe, Jack figured it was to do with the GPF. Max told him he was right, but that he couldn't tell Jack anything about why he was going away.

Nine-year-old Jack Stalwart

Four months ago, Jack received an anonymous note saying: "Your brother is in danger. Only you can save him." As soon as he could, Jack applied to be a secret agent too. Since that time, he's battled some of the world's most dangerous villains, and hopes some day in his travels to find and rescue his brother, Max.

DESTINATION:
New York City
USA

New York City is located on the continent of North America.

•

There are fifty states in the United States of America.

•

New York City is in the state of New York.

•

New York got its name from the British, who named it after the Duke of York.

•

New York City is also known as "the Big Apple."

More than eight million people live in the city.

•

Most of the streets in New York City cross each other at right angles.

•

New York City is home to the Empire State Building, Times Square, and the Statue of Liberty.

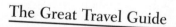

THE ALLOSAURUS:

Everything You Ought to Know

by Lewis Porter

- Dinosaurs first appeared on Earth about 230 million years ago. (The first humanlike creatures appeared on Earth about three million years ago).

- The allosaurus appeared in the late Jurassic period, about 150 million years ago and was one of the largest and most common predators.

- It usually hunted in packs.

- The name allosaurus means *different lizard*. It's pronounced *al-o-saw-rus*.

- A typical allosaurus was ten feet high, thirty-two feet long, and weighed two tons.

- The dinosaurs died out about sixty-five million years ago at the end of the Cretaceous period. No one knows why, but some people think it was because an asteroid hit Earth.

SECRET AGENT GADGET INSTRUCTION MANUAL

Virtual Projection
Camera: Excellent for fooling bad guys into thinking you or something else is somewhere when you're not.

Just type in what you want to project and turn it on. An image will appear up to thirty feet away with the right look, smell, and sound. No one will know it's not for real.

Neutralizing Spray:

When you want the smell of you or something else to go away, the GPF's Neutralizing Spray is your best defence.

Just spray it on and within seconds any trace of your smell totally vanishes. Perfect when you've got meat-eating animals on your trail.

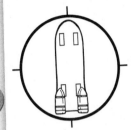

Flyboard: For help getting somewhere faster than your feet will take you. Looks like a skateboard but has two hydrogen jets mounted on the back. Just snap it together (it comes folded in half) and hop on. Push the word *air* on your Watch Phone to make it fly, *blades* to skate on ice, or *wheels* to speed on the ground. After use, every secret agent must return it to GPF headquarters for hydrogen refuelling.

    FLYBOARD PROTOTYPE: CURRENT RESTRICTIONS
    Maximum lift height: 1 meter
    Maximum speed: 25 miles per hour
    Maximum usage time: 1 hour

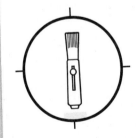

Goo Tube: Perfect for closing up bullet holes and making small repairs. Just lift up the tube with its expanding goo inside and press the ejector button. Instantly, sticky goo will come out and grow, closing the hole.

Chapter 1:
The Mysterious
Package

It was almost 7:15 PM and nine-year-old Secret Agent Jack Stalwart was sitting at his desk, doing his homework, when there was a knock at his bedroom door.

"Who is it?" asked Jack.

"Just me, sweetheart," said a kind voice from the other side.

Jack got up from his desk, walked to his door, and opened it.

"Hi, Mum," he said. "What's up?"

"Just wanted to give you something," she said, handing him a package wrapped in brown paper. "It came for you in today's post."

"Thanks," said Jack, taking the package. It felt as if there were something hard inside.

"That Book of the Month club sure does send you quite a few books," said Jack's mum, pointing to the sender's return address. Jack and his mum looked at the address together. It read: *Great Picks for a Fiver*, or GPF.

"Uh, yes," said Jack nervously, worried his mum might catch on. "They're great," he added. "They always send me just what I need."

"Well," he went on, holding the package close to his chest, "I guess I'd better get on with my homework."

"OK, dear," said his mum as she walked away. "Don't forget to brush your teeth before you go to bed," she added.

Jack shut the door behind his mum and rushed over to his desk. He sat down and carefully unwrapped the package. Inside there was a book with a picture of a dinosaur on the front. It was entitled: *The Allosaurus: Everything You Ought to Know* by Lewis Porter.

The allosaurus, thought Jack. Why are they sending me a book about a dinosaur? And who is this guy, Lewis Porter? He doesn't work for the GPF.

Chapter 2:
The Big Apple

As Jack sat down to think about why the GPF would send him such a thing, a familiar whirring sound came from the corner of his room. It was Whizzy, Jack's miniature globe. Whizzy was starting to spin, as he did almost every night at precisely 7:30 PM.

Jack was a secret agent working for the Global Protection Force, or GPF. His job was to travel the globe defeating evil people or things that threatened the world's most precious treasures. The GPF often sent Jack secret information critical to his next mission through the post. This time they had disguised it as a package from a children's book club.

When Jack was sworn in as a secret agent, the GPF gave him Whizzy. It was a clever way for them to send Jack details about the location of his next mission, because Jack's parents would never know that Whizzy was anything more than a normal globe. As Whizzy started to spin even faster, Jack knew it was only seconds until the GPF and Whizzy revealed where he would be travelling to next.

"Ahem!" Whizzy coughed. A huge jigsaw piece flew out of Whizzy's mouth and sailed past Jack and onto his desk. Whizzy let out a huge sigh of relief. Jack picked up the piece and carried it over to the Magic Map on his wall.

"This one is huge," Jack said to himself. "There are only a few countries in the world this size."

The Magic Map on Jack's bedroom wall was spectacular. It was enormous, with over a hundred and fifty countries carved into it, each with its own shape and color. Jack lifted the piece up to the first possible country. Immediately, the mystery piece slotted in.

"The United States of America!" he gasped with excitement. "I'm going home! But I wonder where in the US I am going. There are fifty states, any one of which could need my help."

Just then a small green light started to appear on the eastern side of the USA. Jack leaned into the map to get a better look. The light was coming from a tiny island inside the state of New York.

"New York City," said Jack. "Fantastic. I'd better grab my Book Bag before I go."

Jack raced over to his bed and pulled out his Secret Agent Book Bag from underneath. He punched in the code of the day – A-P-P-L-E – and checked its

contents. All the GPF's standard

gadgets were there, as well as the
Flyboard and Picture Grabber. He locked
his bag, tossing the straps over his
shoulders, and rushed back to the Magic
Map on his wall. The green light inside
New York City grew brighter and brighter
until it filled his bedroom.

When Jack was ready, he yelled, "Off to
New York City!" And with those words, the
light flickered and burst, swallowing Jack
into the giant map.

Chapter 3:
The Big Toe

When Jack arrived, he found himself
standing in the middle of a great hall. The
sun was shining down from the windows
near the ceiling, and the skeletons of
three massive dinosaurs towered above
him. Jack looked up – way up – at the
dinosaurs and wondered whether any of
the skeletons standing before him were
allosaurus, like in the book he'd received.

"Hmm. Hmm," came a sound from
beside Jack.

He looked to his right and saw a skinny
man with wild, curly blond hair and

9

glasses standing next to him. The man
seemed rather nervous, constantly
shifting his feet and looking over each
shoulder every couple of seconds. His
glasses didn't fit very well, and he spent
most of his time pushing them back up
onto the bridge of his nose.

"You must be Jack," he said, hugging a clipboard close to his chest. "I'm Lewis. Lewis Porter. Thanks for coming," he added, as he extended his hand to Jack and nodded hello. "I'm the one who called the GPF. I am in charge of the dinosaur exhibit here at the museum."

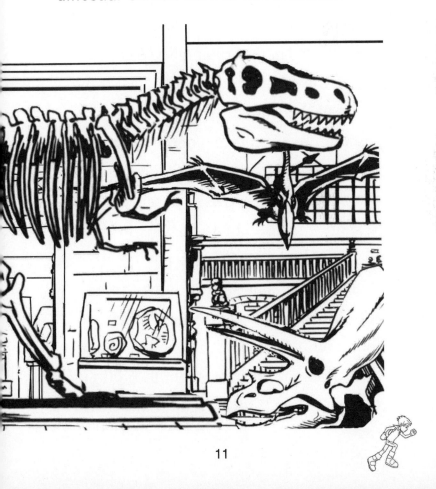

Jack remembered the name on the book from the GPF. The man standing in front of him was its author, Lewis Porter. The only question Jack had now was exactly which museum he was standing in. "The museum?" asked Jack, fishing for more information.

"Yes," said Lewis. "The American Museum of Natural History in New York; one of the most famous museums in the whole of the United States."

Before Jack could respond in any way, Lewis excitedly asked, "Did you get the book on the allosaurus? I asked the GPF to send it to you ahead of time so that you would be fully informed."

"Sure did," said Jack, pulling the book out of his Book Bag. "But I'm a bit confused. I don't understand why I am here. These dinosaurs seem to be doing all right to me," he added, pointing to

the three skeletons standing before
him.

"Are you joking?" responded Lewis, who
seemed genuinely shocked that Jack hadn't
noticed what was wrong. "It's so obvious!"
he gasped, pointing to the smallest of the
three dinosaurs. "Someone has taken the
hallux of this allosaurus!"

"The what?" asked Jack. He had never heard of a hallux before.

"The hallux!" said Lewis in exasperation, his arms flapping excitedly above his head. "Come over here." He yanked Jack towards the allosaurus. "See!" Lewis pointed to where the toe should have been. "The hallux – or first toe – of this dinosaur has been stolen!" he cried.

Jack looked at where the toe should have been. "Are you sure it hasn't just fallen off?" he asked. He didn't want to be rude, but it would be a waste of time if the toe had simply fallen off and rolled underneath something on the floor.

"Things like this don't just fall off," said Lewis. "I know it doesn't look like much, but a missing anything on this dinosaur is a big deal. The allosaurus was one of the most ferocious carnivores of the Late Jurassic. Although it was smaller, it could bring down medium to large plant-eating dinosaurs, like the camptosaurus. It had an expandable jaw that enabled it to chomp down and eat big pieces of meat. It could carry its two-ton body on the strength of its muscular hind legs alone! This skeleton is almost one-hundred-and-fifty million years old. That's why it's important to find the hallux, even if it is one of the skeleton's smaller bones."

"When did you notice it was missing?" Jack asked.

"Last thing yesterday," answered Lewis.

"Was there anyone strange lurking around the dinosaur?" asked Jack.

"Not really," said Lewis. "There were just some school kids on a field trip, like always."

"Well then," said Jack, "the first order of business is to view the footage from your surveillance cameras. Perhaps I can sit in with your security guard while he looks at the tapes."

"That's a great idea," said Lewis. "Let me take you to Hal, who is in charge of surveillance."

"Thanks," Jack said. "And don't worry," he added, trying to reassure Lewis. "I'll find the dinosaur's toe."

"I hope so," Lewis said, sighing as he hugged his clipboard. "Taking care of these dinosaurs is my life."

Before leaving the room, Jack paused to look up at the gigantic skeletons once again. He thought about the TV show he'd recently seen; the one about the life and death of the dinosaurs. Jack shuddered to think what it would have been like to live among them, especially at the time of the allosaurus. The allosaurus was a relative of Tyrannosaurus rex and just as fearsome. Yes, Jack thought, he was glad the

dinosaurs in front of him were a dead
collection of bones.

"Jack," said Lewis, waking Jack from his
thoughts. "Are you ready?" he asked.

"Sure thing," said Jack, hurrying to
catch up with Lewis, who by then had
already left the hall.

Chapter 4:
The Security Meeting

Jack followed Lewis down to the depths of the museum and into a large room filled with high-tech surveillance equipment. In the center of the room was a man wearing a security guard's uniform. He was sitting in a chair in the middle of a circular desk surrounded by at least ten television screens and a panel of controls.

Each TV screen was linked to a digital camera positioned in one of the museum's rooms. All the security officer had to do was push a button and the image on the screen would change to another from a different location. Not only could he watch events as they happened, he could record them. When Jack and Lewis entered the room, Jack noticed that the guard was looking at yesterday's tape.

"Hiya, Lewis!" said the man, a smile widening on his face. "How's it hanging?"

"Uh. All right, Hal," responded Lewis nervously. "This is Jack Stalwart," he said.

"He's going to help me find the allosaurus bone that went missing. Do you mind if he sits with you as you review yesterday's footage?"

"No problem. Come and sit down beside me," said Hal as he pulled up a chair so that Jack could join him.

"Call me if you need me," Lewis said before he left the room.

"Well," said Hal as he punched some buttons, "like I told Lewis, I didn't see anything unusual yesterday. Just some students passing through. Personally, I think Lewis is missin' a few screws – if you know what I mean. He spends way too much time with those bones. I've been looking at these tapes all morning and there's nothing on them to suggest anyone took a thing. Maybe Lewis was cleaning that bone and forgot to put it back or somethin'."

"Maybe," said Jack, "but if Lewis is right, and the toe's been stolen, then we have a crime on our hands. Let's see what's on the video."

Chapter 5:
The Hook

Hal started the digital recording and a black-and-white moving record of the day before was played out before their eyes. They had watched the video for about an hour when Hal turned to Jack.

"See, I told you," he said, pointing to the screen. "Just a bunch of school kids on a field trip."

Jack looked at the monitor. There was indeed an outing of school children whose teacher was showing them the magnificent dinosaur skeletons. As Jack studied the tape, he noticed something strange. One of the boys in the group lingered behind and reached out quickly towards the dinosaur. He then bent down to his school bag and put something inside before standing up to join the group again. At one point, he looked towards the camera.

"Wait," said Jack to Hal. "Can you rewind that section and play it again? But now," he requested, "can you play it one frame at a time?"

"You got it," said Hal.

As Hal played the video in slow motion, Jack leaned in to get a closer look. This time he watched the boy carefully. As he watched, Jack couldn't believe his eyes. The boy had taken a long thin hook out of his jacket and yanked the toe off the dinosaur! He then put it in his school bag.

"I don't believe it!" said Hal. "How did that get past me? I didn't see that happen."

"It would have been hard to see," said Jack, wrinkling his brow. "This kid is clever and fast."

Jack unlocked his Secret Agent Book Bag and took out the Picture Grabber. It was a slim, rectangular silver box that, when plugged into the back of a computer or TV, could take a still picture of whatever was on the screen and print it out in your hand.

"Now, can you pause the video just at the point where he turns towards the camera?" Jack plugged the Picture Grabber into the back of the monitor and pushed the *grab* button. Instantly, it registered the image of the boy. Jack hit the *print* button and a picture printed out from the side of the box.

"Do you know what school he goes to?" asked Jack as he studied the boy's face.

"From the looks of the uniform, I'd say it was East Side Grammar School," answered Hal. "It's located at the intersection of 23rd Street and Park Avenue."

"Great," said Jack, putting the picture of the boy in his pocket. "Thanks for your help. Looks like East Side Grammar School is my next stop."

Chapter 6:
The Halls of Science

As Jack approached the towering steps of East Side Grammar, he paused for a moment to check his Watch Phone. It was just before 8:45 in the morning and, if it were anything like his school in England, classes were about to start.

Boys and girls were hurriedly climbing the steps. As they passed by Jack, he looked carefully at their red, green, and gray clothes and compared them to the uniform on the boy from his picture. Yes, Jack thought, there was no doubt. The boy who took the bone from the museum was definitely a student at this school.

Trying to blend in with the others, he followed the students up the stairs and through the large red wooden doors. Amidst the clang of student lockers, Jack spied a sign that said PRINCIPAL'S OFFICE. There was an arrow on it pointing to the left. Following it, Jack came to a door with

PRINCIPAL
JUDITH
DANNER

a name on it — PRINCIPAL JUDITH DANNER. He knocked twice.

A stern voice answered. "Yes?"

Slowly, Jack opened the door. Sitting at the desk was a woman wearing a bright purple dress. "Principal Danner?" he asked.

"Yes. Who's asking?" she replied, peering over her glasses and sizing up Jack. "You don't look as if you attend East Side Grammar School."

"No, ma'am, I don't," answered Jack.

"My name is Jack Stalwart," he explained, showing his badge. "I work for an international organization called the Global Protection Force. I've been asked to trace the whereabouts of a dinosaur bone that was stolen from the Museum of Natural History. I have reason to believe that the person who took it attends this school."

"One of my students?" said a surprised Principal Danner.

"Yes," explained Jack, showing her the picture of the boy. "I believe this student took one of the toe bones from an allosaurus skeleton yesterday while on a field trip at the museum. I got this picture from the surveillance video."

Principal Danner studied the picture. She shook her head. "I can't believe it. It's Thomas Eberly. One of our finest science students. For the last two years, Thomas has won our school science fair. The entire school is waiting to view this year's entry. His project last year, 'The Survival of the Roach Through the Ice Age,' won him top honors. He even took second prize at the state science-fair competition."

"Do you know what class he's in right now?" asked Jack. "I need to speak to him."

"Unfortunately," replied Principal Danner, "Thomas isn't at school today. He's home sick with the flu."

"I still need to speak to him," said Jack. "Do you have his address?"

"Normally, I wouldn't give out this information. But, as you work for the GPF . . ." Her voice trailed off as she looked for Thomas's information. "Here it is," she said, pulling a piece of paper out of one of her filing cabinets. "He lives in an apartment on 33rd Street, where it crosses Park Avenue. Just ten blocks north of here."

"Thanks, Principal Danner," said Jack as he turned towards the door. "I appreciate your help."

As he left her office, Jack couldn't help but think about this boy named Thomas. He wondered if there was any link between this kid's science project and the missing toe bone.

There's only one way to find out, thought Jack as he hurried through the school and towards the steps outside.

Chapter 7:
The Experiment

As Jack bounded down the steps and onto Park Avenue, he looked out at the street before him. There was a swarm of yellow taxis lining the street and hundreds of people walking around. Horns were honking, people were talking loudly on their mobile phones, and big delivery trucks were making stops in front of shop owners' basement doors. New York City, Jack was realizing, was definitely one of the busiest cities he'd ever seen.

Just then, the ground rumbled. Instinctively, Jack steadied his stance and

grabbed the
straps on his
Book Bag. He
looked through
the grating just
below him and saw
a silver train whizzing
past, under the pavement.
This was the subway – New
York City's underground railway – and
it was heading north through the city, right
underneath Jack's feet.

   Jack continued, up the ten blocks to
Thomas's apartment. He climbed the
stairs in front of the building and went
through a glass door. Stepping into a
small entrance hall, he found himself
facing another glass door. To his right was
a panel on the wall with a series of names
and buttons. Next to the button marked 1B
was the name Eberly. Jack pushed it. A

female voice came over the speaker.

"Hello?" it crackled.

"Hi," said Jack. "My name is Jack Stalwart. I'm here to see Thomas. Principal Danner gave me Thomas's address."

There was a slight pause and then a click. The glass door leading into the building popped open. Jack pushed it further and walked inside, then followed the long hallway until he reached a door marked 1B. Before he could knock, the door was flung open and a friendly woman with an enormously toothy grin stood before him.

"Hi there!" she exclaimed. "I'm Mrs. Eberly. It's so nice of you to come and see Thomas, as he's sick and all. Come on in!"

Jack looked at the woman as she beckoned him inside. She was extremely tall and thin with curly red hair that hung just past her shoulders. It looked as though Jack had interrupted her in the middle of baking something; she was wearing an apron and had flour all over her hands.

"Come and sit down," she added, pointing to a comfortable-looking sofa.

Her accent sounded like Jack's Aunt Millie's. Aunt Millie was Jack's father's sister. She was from Louisiana – one of the states in the southern part of the USA.

She had visited Jack's family in England a few years ago.

"Would you like some juice or somethin'?" she asked Jack.

"Sure," said Jack.

She walked over to the fridge and pulled out a carton of orange juice. As she poured a glass for Jack, she turned to him. "I'm sorry," she said, "what was your name again?"

"Jack," said Jack. "Jack Stalwart," he added.

"I don't remember Thomas ever mentioning your name. Do you and he go to school together?" she asked as she handed over the glass.

"No," said Jack, "we don't go to school together. But Thomas and I have a similar interest in dinosaurs."

"Oh," she said. "You must be in that science club with him. Let me go and tell him you're here."

She walked down the short hallway to the first door on the left and knocked twice. "Thomas," she said, leaning close to the door, "your friend Jack from the science club is here to see you."

A voice came from inside the room. "I don't know any Jack."

"Thomas Eberly," she said, raising her voice, "don't be rude! Now you come out here and see your friend Jack. He's come all this way to visit you."

There was a short pause. Something rustled inside the bedroom. Thomas came out of his bedroom, quickly closing the door behind him. He walked down the hallway towards Jack, who was standing in the kitchen. Thomas, with his red hair and freckles, stood there looking absolutely fine. He didn't look sick at all.

"See," said his mum, pointing to Jack, "Jack has come to see you."

"I don't know this kid, Mom," said Thomas as he stared at Jack. Mrs. Eberly looked over at Jack with a confused expression.

"No," said Jack. "Thomas and I haven't met before. I am here on behalf of the Global Protection Force to collect something he took that doesn't belong to him."

Jack pulled out the picture from his pocket and showed it to Thomas.

Thomas looked at it and then looked at Jack. "Where did you get this?" he asked.

"Don't worry about that," said Jack. "What's important is that you return what you took."

Mrs. Eberly looked even more confused. "What is this all about, Thomas?" she asked.

Just then a loud crash came from the direction of Thomas's bedroom. Then there was a series of barks.

Thomas looked at Jack. "That's just my dog, Freddie," he said, quickly dismissing the noise. "He's just playing in my room." He turned to his mum. "Mom," he went on, answering his mum's earlier question, "I didn't steal anything. I only borrowed it," he said, trying to make a distinction.

"Thomas," said his mum, growing concerned. "What did you take?"

An even bigger crash came from the bedroom now. Then a loud bang, as if something had hit a wall, hard.

"Look, Mom," explained Thomas, "I only borrowed a small piece of bone from the Museum of Natural History yesterday. I was going to return it when I was finished with my science project."

"Thomas Richard Eberly," said the boy's mother angrily, "I can't believe you took something that didn't belong to you. You should know better!"

"GRRRRR . . . GRRRRR . . ." Growling sounds were coming from Thomas's room. Then, out of nowhere, the growl changed to a noise unlike anything the three of them had ever heard before. The force of the sound was so great that it shook the entire building and almost knocked them off their feet.

"RRRRRRRRRRRRRRROOOOOOOOOOOOO-AAAAAAAAAARRRRRRRRRRRRRRR!"

"Thomas!" his mum yelled, scared half out of her wits. "What was THAT?"

Thomas gulped. He looked frightened not only by the noise, but also by the inevitable scolding he was going to get from his mum.

The sound came booming from the room again.

"RRRRRRRRRRRRRROOOOOOOOOOOOO-AAAAAAAAAARRRRRRRRRRRRRRR!"

Thomas's eyes darted towards his room. "Um," he said nervously, "that's this year's science project, Mom."

CRASH! There was a splintering noise from Thomas's bedroom.

"RRRRRRRRRRRRRROOOOOOOOOOOOO-AAAAAAAAAARRRRRRRRRRRRRRR!"

Jack looked quickly round the corner.

Whatever it was had blown Thomas's door clear out of its frame. All that was left were thousands of wooden splinters strewn across the carpet in the hallway. Jack could hear something moving. He waited to see what it was.

Slowly, an enormous green head lowered itself through what used to be the doorway, and into the hallway. It was so massive that it barely fitted through the door frame. Its eyes, which were black and bulging, were roaming up and down the hall. The hundreds of teeth that lined its wide jaws were tall, thin, and razor-sharp.

It was hungry, Jack thought, not only because it was drooling, but also because it seemed to be sniffing for prey. Based on the size of the head alone, Jack reckoned that the creature was about three feet taller than a fully grown man.

"RRRRRRRRRRRRRROOOOOOOOOOOOO-
AAAAAAAAARRRRRRRRRRRRRRRR!"

Its fearsome roar made Jack jump.
Although he hadn't yet seen its body, Jack
recognized the head from Lewis Porter's
book. It was the head of the most
ferocious carnivore of the Late Jurassic. It
was the allosaurus. And Thomas had
brought it to life in his very own bedroom.

Chapter 8:
The Escape

"Under the kitchen table!" Jack screamed as he yanked Thomas and his mum out of the creature's sight.

"RRRRRRRRRRRRRROOOOOOOOOOOOO-AAAAAAAAAARRRRRRRRRRRRRR!"

The frame around Thomas's bedroom door came down with a crash. There wasn't much time. The dinosaur had broken through and was walking on its hind legs down the Eberlys' hallway. It seemed to be growing by the second.

THUD. THUD. THUD. It was coming closer.

SNIFF. SNIFF. It was trying to pick up their scent.

From their hiding place, Jack reached into his Secret Agent Book Bag and pulled out a can of Neutralizing Spray. The GPF's Neutralizing Spray got rid of any scent, whether human or animal. Perfect protection, Jack thought, against meat-

eating dinosaurs. Jack quickly sprayed
himself, Thomas and Mrs. Eberly, just as the
dinosaur made its way to the kitchen. Mrs.
Eberly was trying very hard not to scream.

Jack risked a look from underneath the
tablecloth. The allosaurus hadn't smelled
a thing. It moved past them towards the
front door.

THUD. THUD. THUD. It looked as if it knew where it was going.

CRASH! It slammed against the front door, knocking it down. BLAM! It thundered down the hallway outside and broke through the main entrance, then made its way out onto the street.

"RRRRRRRRRRRRRROOOOOOOOOOOOO-AAAAAAAAAARRRRRRRRRRRRRRR!"

From where they were hiding, Jack could hear the screams of frightened New Yorkers as they encountered the unbelievable sight of a dinosaur running toward them. Mrs. Eberly's eyes were wide with shock. She couldn't speak. Thomas had brought back to life one of the most ferocious dinosaurs in history. And now it was loose on the streets of New York City.

Chapter 9:
The Hope

Once the dinosaur had left the building, Thomas jumped out from beneath the table.

"WOW!" he exclaimed. "I can't believe I did it! I turned my dog, Freddie, into a living, breathing allosaurus! All I had to do was isolate the dinosaur's DNA from the toe bone, mix it with a quickening solution, and give it to Freddie. The transformation was almost instantaneous. No one has ever been able to extract DNA from dinosaur fossils. I'm definitely going to win first prize now!"

"Are you crazy?" Mrs. Eberly shouted. "That thing could have killed us! You should be ashamed of yourself for not thinking of the damage it will cause!"

Thomas looked at his mum and then at Jack, both of whom were wearing grave expressions.

"I'm sorry," said Thomas, looking sheepishly at the ground. He was starting to regret what he'd done. "Am I grounded?"

"Grounding you isn't punishment enough!" his mother yelled. "I'm sure the police'll be knockin' on our door when they find out it was you who created this . . . this . . . THING!"

Thomas looked pale. "If it helps," he offered, holding up a vial with clear fluid inside, "I developed a reversal serum that will change the dinosaur back into Freddie. We just need to get close enough to make him drink it."

Jack quickly grabbed the reversal serum out of Thomas's hand.

"Right," he said, "I'll take this and give it to the allosaurus. You stay here," he told Thomas. "I'll call you when it's safe to join me."

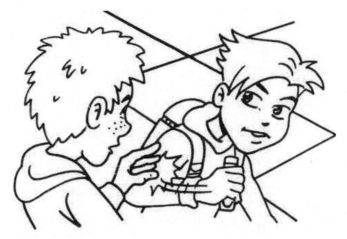

"You mean I can't come?" said Thomas, trying to make Jack feel bad. "After all, it's my dog, Freddie, that's trapped inside that monster."

Jack thought for a second about what to do. He wondered whether Max had ever taken a civilian with him on one of his missions. Bringing someone who wasn't a secret agent was always a risky thing to do. But bringing Thomas, Jack reasoned, could be a good thing. Thomas knew New York City better than Jack. He also probably knew more about the allosaurus. Most of all, he had a relationship with his dog. If there was any of Freddie inside this terrible monster, Jack might just need Thomas to help him out.

"All right," said Jack reluctantly. "You can come, too, but you need to do exactly as I say and stick close to me."

"Cool!" said Thomas eagerly as he bounded towards the hole in the wall that used to be his front door.

"Y'all be careful, OK?" said Mrs. Eberly, looking concerned.

"Don't worry," said Jack, trying to reassure her. "Thomas is in good hands. I won't let anything happen to him."

Mrs. Eberly sighed and then smiled. Jack nodded to her and raced out of the apartment. Then Thomas gave his mum a big hug and dashed out behind Jack. In the distance, a huge roar sounded out across the city.

Chapter 10:
The First Encounter

Jack and Thomas bolted down the steps
and onto the pavement. Jack looked to
the left and then to the right, but there
was no sign of the dinosaur anywhere. The
only indication that the dinosaur existed
were the huge pieces of glass strewn
everywhere from when it had burst out of
the Eberlys' building and onto the street.

Suddenly there was a loud roar. The
dinosaur was still close by.

"Quick!" said Jack to Thomas. "We
need to get the reversal serum into the
allosaurus before it's too late!"

Jack and Thomas dashed round the corner and onto 34th Street. In the middle of the road was the dinosaur. It was frantically swooping down as it ran in an attempt to gobble up people before they could get away. They were screaming as they fled from the monstrous creature.

"Help us!" yelled a man.

"Don't hurt my baby!" shrieked a woman.

The boys raced towards the allosaurus. Up ahead, Jack noticed a man standing still on the pavement. It was as if he were too scared to run. The dinosaur noticed him too and turned to walk in his direction. It began to stalk him step by step, and when it reached him it flashed its daggered teeth as if to say, "Now I am going to eat you."

"Help me!" yelled the man, to anyone who could hear him.

"Stay where you are and don't move!"

Jack shouted. Not that he was going anywhere – the man's legs seemed to be glued to the spot.

The dinosaur took a step back and then forward again. It began to sniff the man and stomp excitedly from side to side.

The only way Jack could save the man was to distract the dinosaur with the prospect of a tastier meal. Thinking quickly, he yanked the Virtual Projection Camera out of his Book Bag. Although it resembled a small video camera, it could project images that looked and smelled like the real thing. Remembering Lewis Porter's book, he lifted up the camera and punched in the word *camptosaurus*.

Instantly a

virtual image of the plant-eating dinosaur appeared on a white wall just a few feet from the frightened man.

The allosaurus stood up on its hind legs as soon as it smelled the camptosaurus. It quickly forgot about the man and began to stalk the other dinosaur. The monster bellowed at the camptosaurus and then opened its jaws wide before snapping them shut with a great big *CHOMP!* Its front teeth hit the brick wall hard, sending

one of them into the air and onto the
pavement with a *CHINK!*

"That must have hurt," said Thomas.

"RRRRRRRRRRRRRROOOOOOOOOOOOOAA
AAAAAAARRRRRRRRRRRRRRR!"

The allosaurus wasn't happy.

"You stay here," said Jack to Thomas as
he left Thomas's side and ran as fast as
he could towards the man.

"Run!" Jack yelled, and he shoved the
man out of harm's way. The shock of

being pushed seemed to wake the man's legs and he quickly dived into a restaurant on the corner.

Jack stood there panting. He looked over at Thomas, who was way down the block. Thomas was trying to tell him something. Jack squinted his eyes and tried to read Thomas's lips. It looked as if he was saying, "Wash out."

Just then, an awful smell wafted into Jack's nose. It smelled like the stench of a thousand rubbish bags that had been sitting out in the sun all day. Slowly, Jack turned and looked out of the corner of his eye. He gasped in fright. The allosaurus had snuck up behind him and was breathing hot dinosaur breath all over him. Instead of the man he had saved, now *Jack* was face-to-face with the most terrifying creature that he had ever seen.

"RRRRRRRRRRRRROOOOOOOOOOOOOAA
-AAAAAAARRRRRRRRRRRRRR!"

Chapter 11:
The Goo

The dinosaur's powerful roar blew Jack off his feet and backward onto the street. He landed on his back and hit his head hard on the pavement. A throbbing pain shot through his skull and he wondered if he had actually cut it open. But thankfully he hadn't.

The dinosaur crept forward and leaned down towards Jack. *SNIFF. SNIFF.* It was trying to tell whether Jack was dead or not. Jack, even in his dazed state, knew that it was only a matter of time before the dinosaur attacked him. He needed to do something – and fast.

Jack gathered his wits and counted to three. He shut his eyes and rolled over twice, swiftly crawling to his knees. Keeping his gaze fixed on the allosaurus, he reached backwards into his Book Bag and pulled out a long tube. This was the GPF's Goo Tube – a perfect solution to Jack's current problem.

The Goo Tube had a glue-like substance hidden inside that, when ejected, expanded on impact. Usually Jack used the Goo Tube to plug holes. As the dinosaur's mouth was as good a hole as any, Jack lifted the tube to face the creature and pushed the ejector button.

The expandable goo flew into the dinosaur's mouth, just as it opened its jaws. *BLOOP! POP!* The goo blew up in an instant so that the dinosaur couldn't close its chops. There was no way it could bite

into Jack now. Jack sprinted back to Thomas.

"That was close!" exclaimed Thomas.

"Thanks for the warning," said Jack, giving Thomas a friendly slap on the back. Jack thought a bit better of Thomas for trying to help him. Maybe he was all right after all.

Jack and Thomas dashed into a nearby launderette and looked at the dinosaur through the glass front door. The sound of tumbling dryers and washing machines rumbled in the background as Jack watched the dinosaur rapidly eating through the goo. It smacked its lips and then headed further along 34th Street.

"What's up ahead?" Jack asked Thomas.

"The Empire State Building," said Thomas, looking worried.

Jack knew that the Empire State Building was one of the most famous buildings in

New York City. Hundreds of people usually waited outside to get into the building and up to the observation deck, and the dinosaur was headed straight for them. How was he going to save so many people at once?

Jack thought about his brother Max and the advice Max used to give him.

"A successful secret agent," Max used to say, "clears his mind first and then thinks of a plan."

Jack did exactly as Max told him. He took a deep breath and considered the risky situation ahead. Almost immediately, an idea popped into his brain.

"Got it!" he said to himself, pleased that he'd come up with a way to distract the monster. Now it was time to put his plan into action, before the dinosaur ate its first victim.

Chapter 12:
The Dreamy World
of Biscuits

Jack turned to Thomas.

"Do you have any dog biscuits on you?"
he asked.

"Huh?" said Thomas, with a confused
expression on his face. "Um. Yeah, I do,"
he answered.

"Great," said Jack. "Let me have them."

Thomas rifled through his trouser
pockets and pulled out a half-eaten bag of
dog biscuits. He handed it to Jack, who
threw it on the ground and began to
stamp all over it.

Thomas scratched his head, wondering what on earth Jack was up to.

"Perfect," said Jack as he picked up the bag of dog-biscuit dust. "Just what I need. Let's get going."

Jack shoved open the launderette door and raced down the street toward the allosaurus, with Thomas following close behind. Up ahead, as Jack had expected, there was a line of people waiting to enter the Empire State Building. The dinosaur was running their way.

"RRRRRRRRRRRRRROOOOOOOOOOOOO-AAAAAAAAAARRRRRRRRRRRRRR!"

It announced its presence. The terrified people turned and started squealing.

Jack reached into his Book Bag. He pulled out the Spray Gun and grabbed an empty vial that was clipped to its side. Then he poured the dog-biscuit dust into the tube and inserted it into the gun. He closed the latch and pointed it into the sky ahead of the dinosaur. Jack pulled the trigger and a spray of biscuit dust was ejected to the right of the dinosaur's path.

As soon as it smelled the biscuits, the allosaurus stopped in its tracks. It looked as if there was a bit of Freddie in it after all! Its enormous tail was wagging excitedly and it dreamily began to run right into the biscuit dust and away from the line of people. Freddie the dinosaur was sniffing in all the biscuit vapors he could.

Quickly, Jack and Thomas ran towards the terrified people and hurried them into a nearby department store. From inside the store, they watched the allosaurus stand up. It shook its head and came out of the trance. The dinosaur looked around to find no one left on the street. Just like a dog, it cocked its leg on a nearby fire hydrant and then moved along 34th Street until it hit Broadway, where it moved north.

Jack pulled out his map of New York City. It looked as though the dinosaur was heading towards 42nd Street and Times Square, one of the most populated places in the city. They were at least ten blocks away from Times Square. There was no way that he and Thomas could keep up with the allosaurus for ten blocks. They needed help. They needed the Flyboard.

Chapter 13:
The Flyboard

Jack ran outside. He reached into his Book
Bag and pulled out the GPF's Flyboard,
which was one of the newer gadgets in the
GPF's arsenal. It looked like a skateboard
only it had two small hydrogen-powered
jets mounted on the back. He unfolded
the board so it clicked into place, put it on
the ground and stepped on.

"Hop on!" he shouted to Thomas.

Jack punched the *wheels* button on his
Watch Phone and activated the *wheels*
feature. Before he knew it, the jet engines
fired up and he and Thomas were

77

speeding toward the dinosaur that was
now at least six blocks ahead.

"RRRRRRRRRRRRRROOOOOOOOOOOOO-
AAAAAAAAARRRRRRRRRRRRRRR!"

Jack could see the allosaurus in front of
them. It was within minutes of reaching
Times Square.

"Get inside!" he screamed to the people
up ahead. "Get inside!" But Jack was too
far away for anyone to hear him.

"I have to warn them!" he shouted to
Thomas above the noise of the

Flyboard's jet engines. He scrambled
through his Book Bag and reached for
the Warning Gun. Quickly he lifted it up
and looked at the side of the barrel.
There were twenty-six buttons on the
Warning Gun, one for each letter of the
alphabet.

He punched in the phrase D-A-N-G-E-R-
G-E-T-I-N-D-O-O-R-S, pointed the barrel into
the air and pulled the trigger. The letters
shot up one by one like
puffs of smoke, so that the
message could be seen
all over the city.

"That should do it,"
said Jack, smiling at
his quick thinking. He
hooked the Warning
Gun onto one of the
belt loops on his pants in
case he needed it again.

The Flyboard meant they were catching up with the dinosaur. They sailed past 39th and 40th Streets, heading towards 42nd Street and Times Square.

"RRRRRRRRRRRRRROOOOOOOOOOOOO-
AAAAAAAAARRRRRRRRRRRRRRR!"

The dinosaur announced itself as it
entered Times Square. Jack and Thomas
zoomed in just behind it. There were
giant television screens flickering on
the tops of buildings. Cars were pulled
to the side of the road with their doors
open and no one left inside. Everyone
must have seen Jack's message. Jack
was pleased. The dinosaur looked
disgusted.

"RRRRRRRRRRRRRROOOOOOOOOOOOO-
AAAAAAAAARRRRRRRRRRRRRRR!"

In its rage, the dinosaur trampled over
several yellow New York taxis. CRUNCH!
PING! The sound was almost deafening as
metal and glass flew all over the road.
Jack and Thomas ducked to avoid the
spewing debris. When the noise stopped,
Jack and Thomas lifted their heads. The

dinosaur was running north again, towards the upper parts of the city.

"Where do you think it's headed?" Jack asked Thomas.

"Well, if it were Freddie," said Thomas, "probably Central Park."

"Why Central Park?" asked Jack.

"Because," Thomas explained, "Freddie loves to visit the animals at the Central Park Zoo."

Jack thought for a minute. It made even more sense that the allosaurus would be heading for the zoo. The animals were mainly kept in cages so they would be easy prey. There would be no way they could escape the dinosaur's powerful jaws. And, of course, they couldn't read Jack's message. They would have no idea that a deadly dinosaur was headed their way.

"Quick!" said Jack. "We have to save the animals!"

Jack fired up the Flyboard once again and he and Thomas jetted off, leaving only a light trail of water-filled steam behind them. They knew it was a race against time, and they had some catching up to do.

Chapter 14:
The Hero

Jack and Thomas sped towards the park.
Up ahead, Thomas spotted the dinosaur.
"It's reached the park!" he screamed. The
two of them watched as its swaying tail
disappeared underneath the trees.

Jack and Thomas ducked as the Flyboard
carried them under the same trees and
onto a road. On the other side of the road
was an enormous ice-skating rink. The
dinosaur was already there and about to
cross it.

"It's crossing the ice!" yelled Thomas as
the dinosaur slammed through a glass

barrier and stepped onto the cold, hard rink. Thankfully for Jack, the ice rink had just closed for the year, so there weren't any people around.

"RRRRRRRRRRRRRROOOOOOOOOOOOO-AAAAAAAAAARRRRRRRRRRRRRR!"

The allosaurus lumbered across the ice and made it to the other side. It roared again before picking up its feet and moving north, this time across the grass.

Jack and Thomas arrived at the edge of the ice and stopped. There was no way around the rink. They had to cross it, too. Jack activated the *blades* feature on the Flyboard. Instantly, the wheels were sucked inside and two long blades popped down. Jack fired up the jets and the Flyboard carried them across the ice at top speed, faster than any champion speed skater could skate.

As they reached the opposite side of the

rink, the Flyboard began to bleep. Jack
looked down. It was not an encouraging
noise. The power bar was telling him that
there was almost no hydrogen left. There
was no way the Flyboard could carry them
any further. Jack needed to think of
another way.

Quickly, he looked around. To his right,
parked on the road, was a yellow taxi with
a man inside. Jack dashed over to the taxi
and banged hard on the window. The

man, who was cowering inside, jumped in his seat and then peered out. He looked at Jack and reluctantly rolled down the window.

"I need a favor," said Jack breathlessly. "I need you to drive north on this road."

"But, zee dinosaur is out zair!" screamed the man. "I don't vant to be ee-ten!"

"I know," said Jack. "I am trying to capture him. If you help me, you'll be a hero."

"A hee-ro?" said the man, a grin brimming on his face. He paused for a second and then said, "OK, I vill help you."

"Great!" said Jack. "C'mon, get in!" he shouted to Thomas as he opened the passenger door of the taxi and dived into the back seat.

Thomas jumped in behind Jack. The taxi driver started the car and slammed his

foot on the pedal. The car screeched north
after the dinosaur and towards the
helpless animals that had no idea what
was coming their way.

Chapter 15:
The Dilemma

Jack looked out at the park from inside the moving car. In the distance, he could see the dinosaur running through the trees and over the ancient boulders that littered the grass. If it weren't for the taxi driver, Jack would have lost the dinosaur by now, but they were almost neck and neck with it and Jack felt sure that they would beat it to the zoo.

The road curved slightly to the left. "Look!" said Thomas to Jack as he pointed to a building. "That's the zoo."

"Great," said Jack. He leaned toward the

driver. "Can you pull over here, please?" he asked.

The driver veered to the left and brought the car to a dead stop.

Jack flung open the door. "Thanks!" he yelled as he and Thomas bolted out of the car and ran towards the entrance.

THE ZOO IS NOW CLOSED

Jack and Thomas ran past a sign saying THE ZOO IS NOW CLOSED and jumped over the turnstiles. They dashed into the meeting area and looked around. The dinosaur was nowhere in sight. As far as Jack could tell, they had managed to beat it to the zoo.

Jack panted breathlessly and thought about the situation. Central Park was spread over 843 acres. The allosaurus could be anywhere. If Thomas was wrong about where Freddie was heading, Jack might fail in his mission. He had to trap the dinosaur and somehow administer the serum.

As Jack was thinking about what to do, he heard a sound. It was the dinosaur's roar and it was coming their way.

Chapter 16:
The Transformation

Jack told Thomas to run for cover while he prepared for the allosaurus to arrive. He quickly reached into his Book Bag and grabbed a metal canister. Inside the container was another GPF gadget – the Rubber Slide – but Jack didn't need the slide today, just the canister itself. He stood there, with the canister in his hands, and waited for the dinosaur to enter the zoo.

"RRRRRRRRRRRRRRROOOOOOOOOOOOO-AAAAAAAAAARRRRRRRRRRRRRRR!"

The dinosaur ripped through the

entrance and smashed the turnstiles. It
raged into the meeting area where Jack
was standing and paused for a second
while it registered his presence. Jack stood
there, his knees beginning to tremble.

Slowly, the dinosaur pawed its way over
to Jack and lowered its head. It took a
long sniff at Jack and showed him its
razor-sharp teeth. A drip of drool slid off
one of its teeth and splattered onto Jack's
foot. All Jack needed was for the dinosaur
to roar again and his plan could be put
into action.

"RRRRRRRRRRRRRRROOOOOOOOOOOOO-
AAAAAAAAARRRRRRRRRRRRRRR!"

With one swift toss, Jack hurled the
canister in the direction of the dinosaur's
gaping mouth. The metal cylinder wedged
itself at the back of the allosaurus's jaws,
making it impossible for the dinosaur to
close its mouth. The creature stood up

and shook its head violently, trying to loosen the canister.

Quickly, Jack pulled the reversal serum out of his trouser pocket and the Super Sling out of his Book Bag. He placed the vial into the catapult and pulled it as far back as he could. With trembling hands he aimed the vial directly at the dinosaur's mouth and fired. *TWANG!*

The serum shot through the air and landed right on the dinosaur's tongue. As it shook its head, the glass vial slipped underneath the metal can and down the back of the creature's throat. The serum was now inside its stomach and it was only a matter of time before it started to work. Jack and Thomas stared at the creature with horror and hope.

Suddenly, the dinosaur bolted upright as if it had been frozen solid. Jack watched as it swayed to the right and

then to the left before crashing down to
the ground with an incredible *THUD!*

It lay there for only a moment before an
enormous gust of wind blew in from the
east. The violent wind swirled around the

allosaurus and began to turn its bones to
dust. Jack, his eyes wide as saucers,
watched as a second gust of wind came
from the west and carried the dinosaur
dust away in a big *WHOOSH!*

When Jack looked down again, all that

was left was his metal canister, a toe bone, and a cute little dog that was wagging its tail excitedly at the animals across the meeting area.

"Freddie!" Thomas shouted with joy as he ran over to his beloved pet. "I'm so glad you're alive! Thanks to Jack, you're back!"

Freddie licked Thomas's face, then when Jack leaned down to the dog Freddie licked him, too.

In the distance, Jack could hear the sounds of police sirens. They were coming to capture the dinosaur. Jack thought about how shocked they would be to find that it had completely vanished.

He turned to Thomas, who was stroking Freddie's fur. "You know," he said to Thomas, "there's still something you need to do."

"I know," said Thomas, looking a bit

sheepish. "I need to return the toe bone.
Can we do it together?" he asked Jack.
"I'm a bit nervous."

"Sure," said Jack as he and Thomas
stood up.

Jack collected his canister and put the
ancient bone safely in his pocket. Then
the three of them – Jack, Thomas, and
Freddie – made their way west out of the
park and towards the museum.

Chapter 17:
The Apology

The trio climbed the steps of the museum and walked inside. There, atop a ladder, dusting the dinosaur bones, was Lewis Porter.

"Hi, Lewis," said Jack as he and Thomas walked towards him.

Lewis turned round. "Hi, Jack!" he said excitedly, clambering down the ladder. "Any luck? I heard about the commotion on the news. I was tempted to get out onto the streets and see the action for myself, but knowing these dinosaurs as well as I do, I decided to stay indoors."

"You were right to do that," said Jack. "It was a pretty hairy situation. But we got it under control and we – that is, Thomas and I – have something to return."

He pulled the missing toe bone out of his pocket, gave it to Thomas and nudged him forwards. "Thomas, here," Jack said, "has something to say."

"Um . . . Um . . ." Thomas said, looking sheepishly at the ground. "I just wanted to say that I am sorry for taking the bone. I shouldn't have done it. I made a mess of everything. I created a monster that could have killed people. I feel awful."

Lewis didn't say anything. He let Thomas carry on.

"And, well, anyway," added Thomas, "I'd like to repay you by helping out here at the museum. That is, if you'd let me."

Lewis took a few seconds to think and then smiled at Thomas. "Wonderful," he

said. "I could use the help. The police
might even look more kindly on you if
they know you're making amends. Why
don't you start by dusting the dinosaurs?"
Lewis suggested. "You can begin at the
top," he said, pointing to an incredibly tall
ladder, "at the head of the barosaurus."

Thomas looked at the barosaurus and
gulped. "You know," he said nervously,
"um . . . I'm a bit scared of heights."

Lewis looked at Thomas. A grin spread
across his face.

"Well, I guess I'd better be going," Jack said to them. He turned to Thomas and smiled. "Take care of yourself, Thomas. And Freddie, too," he said as he patted Freddie's head.

"Sure will," said Thomas. "Thanks again," he said. "Without your help I don't know what would have happened. I've definitely learned my lesson." He looked a bit sad to see Jack go.

Jack smiled and turned to Lewis. "Are there any maps of the world around here?" he asked.

"Of course," Lewis answered. "Through the main hall and to the left."

Jack said goodbye and walked further into the museum, leaving Thomas to clamber up the ladder, his knees clearly shaking with fear.

After Jack passed by some other exhibits in the museum, he noticed the map of the world that Lewis was talking about. Not as big as his own, mind you, but it would do.

He pulled out a small flag from his Book Bag and stuck it into the map on top of Britain. Instantly, a light began to glow inside the country.

Jack waited for the light to shine brightly before he shouted, "Off to England!" It flickered and burst, sucking Jack into the map and transporting him home.

Chapter 18:
The Last Look

When Jack arrived, he found himself in the middle of his room. The time on the clock was exactly 7:31 PM. Suddenly he remembered something.

"Now where are they?" Jack asked himself as he rummaged through the clothes in the middle drawer of his chest of drawers.

When he spied what he was looking for he pulled them out. After a quick change, he walked over to his full-length mirror and took a good look. There he was, dressed head to toe in the dinosaur pajamas that he'd got for Christmas. There were all sorts of dinosaur images on his PJs, but the one on his shoulder was definitely a picture of an allosaurus.

"A perfect end to this mission," he said, smiling to himself as he walked over to his bed and crawled under the covers.

"'Night, Whizzy," he said to his miniature globe. Then he turned out the light and fell asleep.

The Search for
the Sunken
Treasure:
AUSTRALIA

BOOK ②

The Search for the Sunken Treasure: AUSTRALIA

Elizabeth Singer Hunt

Illustrated by Brian Williamson

WEINSTEIN
BOOKS

For Rachel, Josh, Andy, Suzi, and
all of our Australian friends

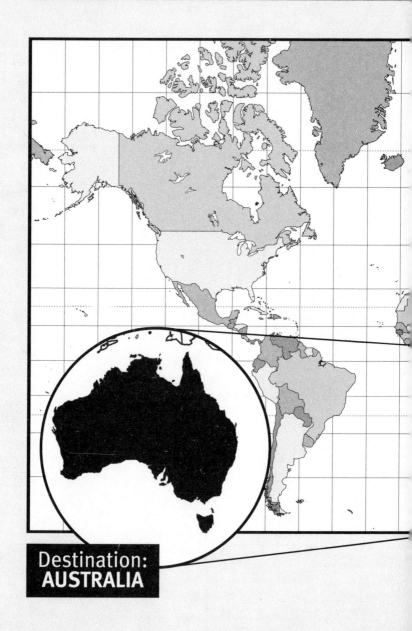

Destination:
AUSTRALIA

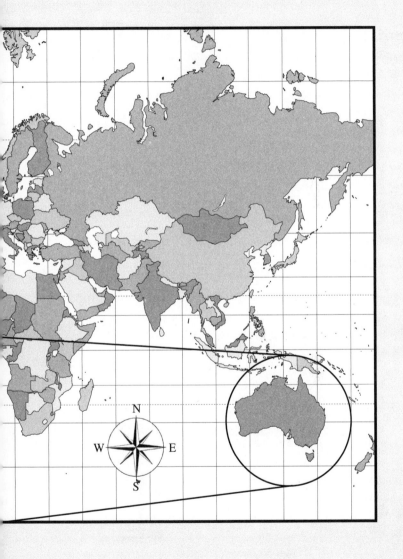

Jack Stalwart applied to be a secret
agent for the Global Protection
Force four months ago.

My name is Jack Stalwart. My older brother,

Max, was a secret agent for you, until he

disappeared on one of your missions. Now I

want to be a secret agent, too. If you choose

me, I will be an excellent secret agent and get

rid of evil villains, just like my brother did.

Sincerely,

Jack Stalwart

Jack Stalwart was sworn in as a Global Protection Force secret agent four months ago. Since that time, he has completed all of his missions successfully and has stopped no less than twelve evil villains. Because of this he has been assigned the code name COURAGE.

Jack has yet to uncover the whereabouts of his brother, Max, who is still working for this organization at a secret location. Do not give Secret Agent Jack Stalwart this information. He is never to know about his brother.

Gerald Barter
Director, Global Protection Force

THINGS YOU'LL FIND IN EVERY BOOK

Watch Phone: The only gadget Jack wears all the time, even when he's not on official business. His Watch Phone is the central gadget that makes most others work. Pushing the *C* button reveals the code of the day – necessary to unlock Jack's Secret Agent Book Bag. *T* tells him the position of his Transponder device. *L* confirms his location in the world. There are buttons on both sides, one of which ejects his lifesaving Melting Ink Pen. Beyond these functions, it also works as a phone and, of course, gives Jack the time of day.

Global Protection Force (GPF): The GPF is the organization Jack works for. It's a worldwide force of young secret agents whose aim is to protect the world's people, places, and possessions. No one knows exactly where its main offices are located (all correspondence and gadgets for repair are sent to a special PO Box, and training is held at various locations around the world), but Jack thinks it's somewhere cold, like the Arctic Circle.

Whizzy: Jack's magical miniature globe. Almost every night at precisely 7:30 PM, the GPF uses Whizzy to send Jack the identity of the country that he must travel to. Whizzy can't talk, but he can cough up messages. Jack's parents don't know Whizzy is anything more than a normal globe.

The Magic Map: The magical map hanging on Jack's bedroom wall. Unlike most maps, the GPF's map is made of a mysterious wood. Once Jack inserts the country piece from Whizzy, the map swallows Jack whole and sends him away on his missions. When he returns, he arrives precisely one minute after he left.

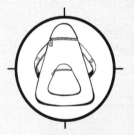

Secret Agent Book Bag: The Book Bag that Jack wears on every adventure. Licensed only to GPF secret agents, it contains top-secret gadgets necessary to foil bad guys and escape certain death. To activate the bag before each mission, Jack must punch in a secret code given to him by his Watch Phone. Once he's away, all he has to do is place his finger on the zipper, which identifies him as the owner of the bag, and it immediately opens.

THE STALWART FAMILY

Jack's dad, John

He moved the family to England when Jack was two, in order to take a job with an aerospace company. As far as Jack knows, his dad designs and manufactures aeroplane parts. Jack's dad thinks he is an ordinary boy and that his other son, Max, attends a school in Switzerland. Jack's dad is American and his mum is British, which makes Jack a bit of both.

Jack's mum, Corinne

One of the greatest mums as far as Jack is concerned. When she and her husband received a letter from a posh school in Switzerland inviting Max to attend, they were overjoyed. Since Max left six months ago, they have received numerous notes in Max's handwriting telling them he's OK. Little do they know it's all a lie and that it's the GPF sending those letters.

Jack's older brother, Max

Two years ago, at the age of nine, Max joined the GPF. Max used to tell Jack about his adventures and show him how to work his secret-agent gadgets. When the family received a letter inviting Max to attend a school in Europe, Jack figured it was to do with the GPF. Max told him he was right, but that he couldn't tell Jack anything about why he was going away.

Nine-year-old Jack Stalwart

Four months ago, Jack received an anonymous note saying: "Your brother is in danger. Only you can save him." As soon as he could, Jack applied to be a secret agent too. Since that time, he's battled some of the world's most dangerous villains, and hopes some day in his travels to find and rescue his brother, Max.

DESTINATION: *Australia*

Mainland Australia was first settled by Aboriginal people about 50,000 years ago. Many came from Southeast Asia.

•

On January 26, 1788, ships from Great Britain landed in present-day Sydney. They were carrying migrants and convicts. The date of this landing is celebrated in Australia as Australia's National Day.

•

Australia is a diverse continent made up of deserts, tropical rainforests, snow-capped mountains, and forests.

Over twenty million people live on the continent of Australia today.

•

Canberra is the capital city.

•

Australia is divided into six states (New South Wales, Queensland, South Australia, Tasmania, Victoria, Western Australia) and two territories (Northern Territory and Australian Capital Territory).

•

Although Australia has a prime minister, its head of state is the Queen of England (Queen Elizabeth II).

The Great Travel Guide

THINGS EVERY SECRET AGENT SHOULD KNOW ABOUT HMS *PANDORA*

HMS *Pandora* was a British warship.

•

It set sail on November 7, 1790, from Portsmouth, England, in search of men who had hijacked HMS *Bounty*. These hijackers were called mutineers.

•

After finding the mutineers in Tahiti, HMS *Pandora* headed back to England.

•

The ship sank on August 29, 1791, as it hit the Great Barrier Reef during a violent storm. Thirty-five people died, including four of the prisoners.

•

The wreck lies sixty-five nautical miles off the northern coast of Australia and is about a hundred feet below the surface.

•

The front of the boat is called the bow (sounds like *cow*). The back of the boat is called the stern.

SECRET AGENT GADGET INSTRUCTION MANUAL

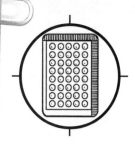

Anti-Puke Pills: Whenever you feel as if you're going to be sick, just pop two of these pills into your mouth and swallow (with water, if available). Its active ingredients will calm the sickness and bring you back to normal within minutes.

Dozing Spray: Perfect when you need to put your enemies to sleep. Just hold the canister up to their nose and push the trigger. A fine mist will filter out of the bottle and into their nostrils, sending them into a deep sleep within seconds.

MAXIMUM DOZE: 10–15 minutes

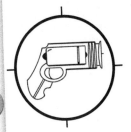

Spray Gun: A handheld gun that secret agents can use to spray liquids found in special tubes. There's one empty tube on the side of the gun and a full set of five tubes in the GPF's Vial Box (see below). Just take the desired tube and insert it into the barrel of the Spray Gun. Pull the trigger to spray the contents over your opponent. You can also switch from *spray* to *syringe* if you needed to inject something.

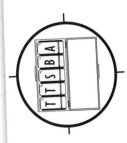

Vial Box: A metal container used to carry the tubes necessary for the Spray Gun. Inside the box are five clear tubes, each filled with a different liquid:

A: antibiotic

B: blood
(matched to the secret agent's blood type)
S: steroid (for temporary muscle power)
T: tranquillizer (x2)

Chapter 1:
The Reef

Eighteen-year-old Alfie Doyle stood at the back of the boat in his favorite blue wetsuit and looked out over the rough Australian sea. He fastened his oxygen tank, put his mouthpiece in, and took a deep breath before jumping off.

SPLASH!

He crashed into the churning waves. Almost instantly, he began to sink. He checked his oxygen levels and glanced at his watch. There was only twenty minutes to swim to the bottom, do a bit of research, and get back to the boat before he ran out of air.

Ready, he tipped his head forward and plunged into the depths. As he descended, he swam past some of the Great Barrier Reef's amazing sea life. There were orange clown fish, purple and yellow surgeonfish, schools of blue-green puller fish, and even brownish moray eels. This was the bit Alfie loved most – swimming with some of the most unusual sea creatures in the world.

Alfie continued downwards. As he approached the seabed, he flicked on his underwater flashlight. When his feet touched the bottom, he lifted his hand to his mouthpiece and switched on his Underwater Communications Piece.

"Touchdown," said Alfie into the UCP. "Will report everything as I go." In his earpiece he could hear Harry, his boss, who was still on the boat.

"Good," said Harry. "Let's hope the sands haven't shifted that much."

Alfie swam to the back of the wreck, or the stern. Last time they were there, he and Harry had discovered some pieces from the officers' quarters. From what Alfie could tell, everything was as they left it forty-eight hours ago.

He carried on, swimming the length of the rotted wooden boat towards the bow at the front. The bow was where the crew members would have lived, and Harry in

3

particular was keen to see what was there. Today their job was to remove the sand covering the bow, bring up any relics, and hand them over to the State Maritime Museum.

As Alfie raised his flashlight to survey the scene, he gasped. The sand that had covered the front of the wreck two days ago was no longer there. He swam a bit closer and noticed a hole going down into the area where the crew members' quarters would have been.

Alfie frantically spoke into his UCP. "Harry, something's wrong!"

"What do you mean?" asked Harry.

"Something's not right," said Alfie. "There's no sand!"

As Alfie was talking, a dark figure in diving gear snuck up behind him. The stranger lifted a gun and pointed a spear directly at him.

"I think someone's taken something from HMS *Pandora*!" said Alfie, his eyes bulging with panic.

Just then, the figure pulled the trigger, releasing the deadly spear into Alfie's leg.

"Owww!" howled Alfie, blinded by the pain.

"Alfie! Alfie!" Harry called into his speaker. But there was no reply, just a crackling noise from Alfie's UCP.

Chapter 2:
The Competition

At the same time, but in a different place, nine-year-old Jack Stalwart stood on top of a square swimmer's block in his lucky blue swim trunks and looked out over the indoor pool. He was in lane number three and about to dive into the most important swimming race of his young life – the fifty-meter breaststroke.

Jack was a member of the Surrey Sharks, the county team of swimmers that had won the national swimming competition for the past five years. It was

Jack's first time representing the Sharks in the breaststroke and he was hoping he wouldn't let them down.

He glanced to his left. In lane four was Rusty Sanders, winner of last year's event. Rusty was bigger and more muscular than Jack and was listed as the county favorite to triumph again this year. Rusty was also a miserable bully.

When Jack and Rusty entered the arena, Rusty spat at him, growled, and called him a loser. Beyond wanting to win for the county of Surrey, Jack wanted to win in order to wipe the smirk off Rusty Sanders's face.

The official walked to the edge of the pool and drew his starting pistol. He lifted it high in the air.

"On your marks," he said loudly. The swimmers bent down to touch their toes.

"Get set," he yelled. Jack took a deep breath.

"Go!" he hollered as he pulled the trigger on the gun, sending a loud, sharp pop through the air.

Jack threw himself forward and dived, head first, into the pool. A thunderous noise entered his ears as he plunged underwater.

Thrusting with his arms, he pulled his head to the surface. He took his first breath and then looked to the side. Rusty was already a body's length ahead.

"Go! Go!" Jack could hear the crowd screaming. With all his might and with every stroke, Jack pulled his hands and arms through the water.

As Jack approached the end of the first lap, he could hear his parents' voices through the crowd.

"Come on, Jack!" his mum cheered.

"You can do it!" hollered his dad.

He slapped his hands against the wall and flung his body back around. While he was underwater, he saw Rusty thundering along in lane four. When Jack's head broke above the water, the crowd noise began to rise.

"Come on, Jack!"

"Let's go, Sharks!"

Jack was really swimming now. His muscles were burning and his arms ached. He was neck and neck with Rusty, their

heads bobbing up and down, and the finish line was only feet away.

With all the strength he could muster, Jack pulled and pushed his arms. When he reached the wall, he slapped his hands hard. Within a fraction of a second, Rusty did, too. But Jack was first. Jack had won! The crowd went wild!

The announcer's voice boomed throughout the arena. "Our new national champion in the fifty-meter breaststroke with a time of thirty-eight seconds is Jack Stalwart!" The supporters roared with delight.

Jack looked over at Rusty and put out his hand for a polite handshake. But Rusty sneered, leaped out of the pool, and made his way towards the locker room. It didn't

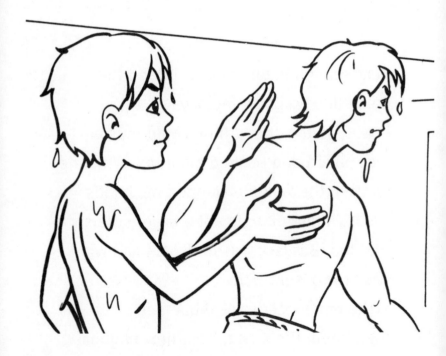

matter to Jack that Rusty was miffed. He'd proven to himself and to Rusty that he was the better swimmer.

Jack looked across the pool at his parents, who were jumping up and down with glee. Then he glanced across to the clock on the wall. It was 7:00 PM.

Yikes, thought Jack. I'd better get changed.

Jack jumped out of the pool and walked across to the boys' changing room. On the way he was grabbed by reporters who wanted his picture for the local paper, the *Surrey Tribune*. Jack smiled politely and posed for the photos. He quickly showered, changed his clothes, and met his mum and dad outside. On the drive home, his parents couldn't stop talking about Jack's triumphant win. But all Jack could think about was the time.

He looked at his Watch Phone. It was

7:20 PM. Luckily for him, his dad knew plenty of short cuts and by 7:26 PM they had pulled into the drive. Pretending he needed a soak in the bath, Jack kissed his parents goodnight and bounded up the stairs. As he opened his bedroom door, the clock in the hall chimed 7:30 PM.

Chapter 3:
The Land of Oz

Closing the door behind him, Jack walked over to his bed. He sat on it for a few seconds thinking how tired he actually was. He hadn't pushed his body that hard in a while and he figured it was going to take some time for it to recover. But, of course, there was never any rest for a GPF secret agent.

Just then, Jack heard a noise from his bedside table. Whizzy, Jack's magical miniature globe, was starting to spin. Whizzy whirled and twirled until he

couldn't do it
any more and
coughed –
Ahem! An
enormous jigsaw
piece in the
shape of a
country spewed
out of his
mouth. Jack bent

down to the floor and picked it up.

Almost immediately, he recognized its
shape. Not only was it the shape of a
country, it was also the shape of one of
the seven continents. There was only one
place in the world that could claim that
honor.

Jack walked over to the giant map of the
world that hung on his wall. Unlike most
world maps that were made of paper,
Jack's was a special one made of wood.

Each one of the 150-plus countries was carved and painted in its very own color. Whenever Jack placed the piece in the right spot, it revealed the location of Jack's next mission and transported him there.

Jack lifted the piece from Whizzy and put it in the lower right-hand corner. Immediately, it slotted in. As expected, the name "AUSTRALIA" flashed in the middle.

Cool! thought Jack. I've never been to Australia before.

He rushed over to his bed and dropped to his knees. He grabbed underneath for his Secret Agent Book Bag. Hitting the C button on his Watch Phone, he accessed the code of the day – R-E-E-F – and keyed it into the lock on his bag. Instantly, it popped opened, revealing a host of gadgets inside. The Oxygen Exchanger, the Morphing Suit, and The Egg were all there.

He threw the bag on his back and tugged the straps tight.

From deep inside Australia, a beautiful blue light began to glow. When the time was right, Jack hollered, "Off to Australia!" and the light burst, swallowing Jack into the Magic Map.

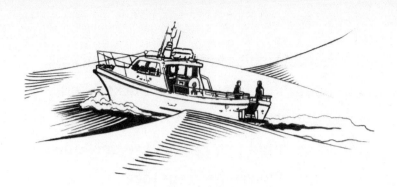

Chapter 4:
The Explorer

When Jack arrived, he found himself on
the deck of a boat that was bobbing up
and down in the middle of the ocean. The
boat lurched forward and a spray of water
leaped from the sea and slapped Jack in
the face.

Funny, Jack thought as he wiped the
water from his eyes, this wasn't the
Australia I was expecting. I was looking
forward to seeing the outback, some
crocs, and a few kangaroos.

SWOOSH!

A horrible noise came from the back of the boat. Immediately, Jack ducked and looked in the direction of the sound. As far as he could tell, he was the only one on board. Slowly, he crept towards the rear and onto a platform hanging from the back. He peered over the edge and into the sea. There was nothing to see but the ocean's dark water. As Jack stared at the waves, he began to feel sick. He reached into his Book Bag and pulled out a packet of Anti-Puke Pills. He popped two into his mouth and swallowed them quickly, so he wouldn't hurl all over the deck.

SWOOSH!

There was the noise again. This time a spray of water shot

up in front of the platform. Jack's eyes widened as a round, black object surfaced from underneath the sea.

The object turned round and then looked at Jack. It was, in fact, a diver's head, and now he was climbing onto the boat. Jack readied himself in case of attack, while the diver climbed onto the platform and took off his mask.

"G'day, mate!" he said, with a smile and a wink. "My name is Harry Pearson," he added, thrusting his hand out towards Jack's. "You must be Jack."

Jack paused and looked at Harry. He was tall and thin with a square-shaped jaw. Seems to be a friendly guy, thought Jack as he put out his hand to join Harry's.

"So," said Jack, his arm wobbling at the force of Harry's shake, "what seems to be the problem?"

"Well," said Harry, sighing as he took off his equipment. "We could use your help. You see," he explained, "the boat that we're on is called the *Explorer*. I'm part of a team of divers researching the shipwreck of HMS *Pandora*. It sank here on the Great Barrier Reef over two hundred years ago. We're in the process of recovering its treasures. I say treasures, mind you, but there's no gold. Just pieces of naval history that the local museum is interested in," Harry carried on. "We dived down two days ago and retrieved some interesting bits from the stern. Today we were set to descend to the bow, but we've hit a snag."

"What kind of snag?" asked Jack.

"Well," answered Harry, "one of my best divers, Alfie Doyle, went down to survey the condition of the wreck this morning. While he was down there he radioed up that he thought someone had taken something from the wreck."

"What did they take?" asked Jack.

"That's the problem – I don't know," said Harry.

"Well, where's Alfie?" said Jack.

"That's problem number two," said Harry. "Alfie's gone. Totally vanished. I lost all contact with him at 09:00 hours. Could have been a shark attack, of course, but I've just been down to look for his equipment and there's nothing. It's rare for a shark to eat a diver's oxygen tank, so I'm really not sure what to think."

"That is pretty odd," agreed Jack.

"That's why I called the GPF," said Harry. "To find Alfie and to figure out what on earth happened down there."

"I'll get to the bottom of this," said Jack, trying to reassure Harry. "The first thing we ought to do is take a look at the wreck. There might be a clue that answers both questions."

"Great," said Harry. "Give me a few minutes to get some more oxygen. Are you a good swimmer?"

"I'm pretty good," Jack answered. "I can swim with the Sharks." He smiled, thinking of his Surrey Sharks swimming team.

"Well, given what's happened this morning," Harry said, "let's hope we don't get the pleasure of doing that!" With that, he walked towards the bow, leaving Jack on the platform to stare down at the sea below.

Chapter 5:
The Preparation

After a few minutes, Harry returned, carrying a small wetsuit, a mask, and a couple of oxygen tanks. "Here," he said, passing them to Jack. "These should fit you."

"Thanks anyway, Harry," Jack said. "But I've brought my own equipment."

Harry looked at Jack, who was dressed in a pair of trousers and a shirt. "Well," he said, furrowing his brow, "where are you hiding it? In your underwear?"

"In here," said Jack, pointing to the Book Bag on his back.

Jack slipped off his Book Bag, reached inside, and pulled out a small round device that was no bigger than his hand. Coming out of its right side was a long tube that reached around and then went back into another hole on the left.

This was the Oxygen Exchanger – the most exclusive device for underwater agents. It could turn the air that someone breathed out into fresh oxygen, so there was no need to have a tank.

Jack then reached into his Book Bag and pulled out a sheet of flexible black plastic. This was the GPF's Morphing Suit. He wrapped the material around his body and almost instantly it molded to form a diver's wetsuit, complete with flippers.

"Wow," said Harry, clearly impressed.

Lastly, Jack pulled a pair of the GPF's Google Goggles from his bag and put them on. Unlike ordinary swimming goggles, these had a built-in zoom lens that enabled secret agents to see far into the distance when they were underwater.

Jack picked up his Oxygen Exchanger and flung his Book Bag over his shoulders. He tugged on the straps and looked at Harry. "Well, I'm ready to go," he said.

Harry, still amazed at Jack's gadgets, stammered, "You . . . ah . . . ah, forgot something." He pointed to Jack's back. "That bag is going to get soaked."

"Nope," said Jack with a smile on his face. "It's waterproof."

Harry shook his head and slipped his new oxygen tanks onto his back. He put his mask on his face and walked over to the edge of the platform, then turned back to Jack. "OK, young man," he said. "Let's hope those fancy gadgets of yours really work." He put his breathing apparatus into his mouth, then stepped off the side.

Jack walked over to where Harry had been. He put his Oxygen Exchanger on, took a deep breath and jumped into the stirring sea towards the mystery that lay below.

Chapter 6:
The Wreck

Harry was farther down than Jack, looking
back at him and pointing to a bright
yellow rope that hung from the back of the
boat and down through the ocean. Jack
knew that Harry was trying to tell him to
follow the rope so he wouldn't get lost. It
was a clever trick that lots of divers use.

As they descended, Jack looked at his
Watch Phone. It had switched to *location*
mode, telling him he was fifty feet under
the surface of the sea. Jack continued to
follow Harry past the jagged corals of the

Great Barrier Reef. He had read about
the reef in books at home, but he couldn't

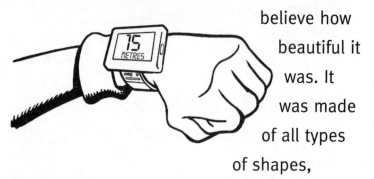

believe how
beautiful it
was. It
was made
of all types
of shapes,

colors, and patterns and almost every part
of it was lived in by some colorful piece of
sea life.

As Jack and Harry approached eighty-two
feet, the reef started to disappear, and
Jack could see the seabed below. There,
covered mostly by sand, was the wreck of
HMS *Pandora*. Jack understood why Harry
thought it was so special. It was awesome
– a mass of timber and iron covered by
glittering sand, and lying peacefully on the
ocean floor. Harry pointed to the stern to
tell Jack where they had already been.

Then he pointed to the bow to show where Alfie had gone missing.

Jack swam in to get a closer look. According to Harry, Alfie had said that the sand had been removed and there was a hole into the boat. Sure enough, it looked as if the bow of the *Pandora* had been disturbed. But where was Alfie? There was no sign of him or any of his equipment.

The only way to figure out what had happened was to use the GPF's Time Capture device – a gadget that could play back events that had happened underwater up to two hours before. It did this by tracking the heat left behind from the objects that were there. The Time Capture was even clever enough to tell Jack whether the object was a human, fish, or other type of creature. Red meant human; orange meant fish; and blue meant there was a shark on the scene.

When he was ready, Jack waved Harry over. He turned on the Time Capture, pointed it towards the bow, and set the time to just before Alfie disappeared, about two hours ago. As Jack and Harry stared at the device, a series of objects appeared on the screen.

At first there were only small orange blobs. Then an enormous red object came

into view and began to linger over the bow. Harry nodded to say that this must have been Alfie doing his work. Within minutes another red figure swam up to the first. There was a struggle between the two, then they both swam away.

Jack sighed and looked at Harry. They knew this wasn't a shark attack. When the figures had left the screen they had swum away from the wreck and to the left. Jack put the Time Capture away and then twisted the rim of his Google Goggles to the maximum length setting. His vision through his Google Goggles cut through the sea. Jack could now see up to sixty-five feet ahead. He scanned the water, looking for any sign of Alfie. But there wasn't a human in sight.

He motioned to Harry that they had to rise. As quickly as they could, they began to swim to the surface. Jack thought about what he had seen on the Time Capture. Because the color of Alfie's figure continued to stay red, there was hope that Alfie hadn't been killed on the spot.

But whoever did this was a dangerous person. He or she was obviously trying to keep whatever they took from HMS *Pandora* a secret. Jack needed to be careful. There were predators in the reef other than the creatures that lived down there and no doubt he was going to come face to face with one pretty soon.

Chapter 7:
The Klan

As soon as Jack and Harry surfaced, Jack crawled out of the water and onto the platform. He took the Oxygen Exchanger out of his mouth and faced the direction that Alfie and his attacker were headed. He twisted the rims of his Google Goggles again, and his vision shot through the air.

He scanned the top of the water and noticed a small cay – a tiny island of sand – approximately three miles from the *Explorer*. Usually there was nothing

on a cay, but on this particular one there
was something strange.

Anchored nearby was a large wooden
boat. Rising from the decks were three tall
masts with climbing nets along the sides
and a crow's nest at the top of the middle
mast. On deck, several large men were
chatting, while others with tattoos on
their arms wheeled goods down a plank

and onto the beach. Jack knew exactly
what kind of ship it was.

"A pirate ship!" he yelled with a mix of
horror and delight. He had only ever seen
boats like these in movies and books.

"What do you mean a pirate ship?"
asked Harry.

"You heard me," said Jack. "A real
live pirate ship! Over there, on that
cay." He pointed in the direction of
the boat.

Jack zoomed
in for a
better look.
At the front
of the ship
was a black-
and-white flag.
But it didn't have a
skull and crossed
swords on it – it had

a picture of a Komodo dragon, the world's largest lizard.

This can only mean one thing, Jack thought to himself. "See that flag over there?" he said out loud, handing the Google Goggles to Harry. Harry strapped them on to take a look. "That's the flag of the Komodo Klan," said Jack.

"The Komodo Klan?" said Harry, sounding puzzled. "Who are they?"

"One of the deadliest groups of pirates around," said Jack. "They come from Indonesia, just north of here, and sail the seas between Indonesia, Papua New Guinea, and Australia, looking for treasure. They find it and then sell it to make money. The reason they're so dangerous is that they'll stop at nothing – not even murder – to get what they want."

"And you think they found something valuable in HMS *Pandora*?" Harry asked.

"I do," said Jack. "And I think they took Alfie with them."

"But why would treasure-hunting pirates be interested in HMS *Pandora*?" asked Harry.

"There's nothing down there but bits of naval history like navigation equipment and small personal items belonging to the crew."

"My bet," said Jack, "is that there's more down there than you think. The Komodo Klan is only interested in the three Gs – gold, guns, and gems. They don't waste their time with anything else. Which is why," he continued, "I have to get onto that boat. If Alfie is still alive it's because they think he might know something. And when they find out he doesn't, they will kill him."

Harry gulped. "What can I do?" he asked.

"Stay here," said Jack. "You never know – Alfie might find a way to escape and get back to the boat."

"What are you going to do?" asked Harry. "It's too dangerous for you to go over there alone."

"I'm not worried," said Jack with a confident smile. "All I need is a clever plan and my little boat."

"Your boat?" said Harry, looking confused. "What boat? Don't tell me you have a boat in that bag of yours!"

"Sure do," said Jack, slipping his Book Bag off his shoulders. "And it's one of the best around."

Chapter 8:
The Egg

Jack laid his Book Bag on the deck and pulled out what looked like a plastic toy boat. He walked over to the platform and stood at its edge. He dropped the boat into the ocean and watched as it grew into one of the most advanced mini-submarines available to modern spies. Because of its oval shape, the GPF called it The Egg. Its see-through shell at the top lifted to show Jack the driver's seat inside.

"Keep your eyes open for danger, Harry,"

said Jack as he threw his flippers inside and stepped into the floating pod. "Next time you see me I'll have Alfie and the treasure from HMS *Pandora*."

"Hope so," said Harry, waving goodbye to Jack.

Jack pushed the *close* button on the lid. Knowing that he didn't need to go underwater yet, he set the boat to *cruise* and the silent engines started up. Staying above the water, The Egg edged forward and headed towards the cay in the distance.

Once he was ready, Jack switched from *cruise* to *stealth* and then pushed the *submerge* button. Within seconds, The Egg started to sink and plunged Jack into the waters below.

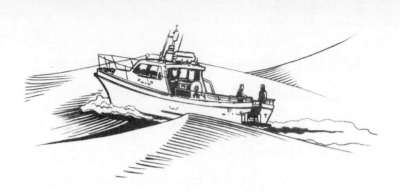

Chapter 9:
The Approach

As The Egg travelled through the ocean, Jack looked at the dashboard. In the middle was a small screen that told him exactly where he was and where he was headed. There was a flashing green light signifying the location of The Egg and a red one marking the Komodo Klan's boat. Jack tapped the screen twice to target the pirate ship. The Egg adjusted its path and headed straight for it.

When he could see he was close enough, Jack turned off the engines and

put his Oxygen Exchanger back on. Then
he programmed his Watch Phone, marking
The Egg's location in case he needed to
find it for an emergency escape. Sliding
his hands along the side of his chair, he
reached for a small lever and yanked it
upwards. Instantly he was ejected feet
first into the water through a hatch
underneath.

Up ahead, he could see the bottom of the pirate ship's hull and the chain of its anchor. He swam to the chain and grabbed onto it tightly. He pulled himself up along it, climbing one link at a time until he reached the surface of the water. He poked his head out of the water and listened carefully.

"Over here, mate!" said a pirate.

"Where?" asked another one.

"Put it on the sand, by the shack," the first replied.

"What are we doing with the kid?" said another voice.

"The boss said to hold onto him until nightfall and then we can kill him," sniggered the first pirate.

Interesting, Jack thought. No one, not even the GPF, knew the identity of the boss of the Komodo Klan. Whoever it was, it was clear that he planned to kill Alfie.

Jack needed to work quickly if he was going to save him.

He switched his Google Goggles from *tunnel vision* to *x-ray* and focused in on the boat itself. There were five pirates on the boat's upper deck, stacking boxes and wheeling some of them down a ramp onto the beach. Almost all

the boxes were plain, but on the one that was sitting on the deck, Jack spied the word *PANDORA*.

Whatever they took from HMS *Pandora* must be inside that box, thought Jack.

Under a hole in the deck, there were several steps leading to a small room. In the middle of the room was a small prison cell clamped shut with a lock. Inside the cell was a person sitting on a chair with his hands tied behind his back. It was Alfie, Jack figured, and he was alive! The Google Goggles could just make out some silver tape over his mouth.

Jack turned his attention from the boat to the cay. There was a small wooden house that looked as if it had been recently built. He could see at least ten people inside. Some were sitting at tables and eating food. A few were watching a small TV while others were working hard to stack the boxes that were coming from the ship. Tilted up against the walls was a collection of rifles and spear guns.

This must be their temporary headquarters, thought Jack. They must be unloading their treasures before moving on.

Between the five on the boat and the ten in the shack, Jack knew he had at least fifteen pirates to deal with. As far as he could tell, none were acting like the Komodo Klan's boss. But there was something else that he noticed – most of the pirates were looking at the shack on the beach. This was the perfect time to make a move.

Chapter 10:
The Boss

Jack used all his energy to pull himself up the anchor chain and over the side of the boat. Putting his Oxygen Exchanger back inside his Book Bag, he scurried across the deck to the hole in the floor, then lowered himself down the steps inside. When he got to the bottom, he looked around. No one and nothing but Alfie was there. He rushed over to the cell and put his finger to his mouth.

"Don't make a noise," he whispered. "Are you Alfie?" The black-haired boy nodded. "My name is Jack," he explained. "I'm here to save you."

But instead of looking relieved, Alfie looked frightened. He was shaking his head violently at Jack. It was as if he were trying to tell him something, but the tape on his mouth was stopping him.

Jack quickly turned around to check the room, but there was no one behind him. He reached into the Book Bag and pulled out his Magic Key Maker. He slotted the thin piece of rubber into the key hole. Instantly, it melted to form the shape of a key, then hardened again in seconds. Jack turned the key to the right and – *snap!* – the lock popped open. He rushed over to Alfie.

With his fingers, he grabbed the edge of the tape covering Alfie's mouth and gently peeled it away. Instead of the thanks he was expecting, a rush of words started to pour out of his mouth.

"Jack!" he whispered in horror. "There are cameras in this room. You need to be careful! They've probably seen you. They'll kill you if they find you in here!"

Almost as soon as Alfie finished warning Jack, a female voice came from over by the stairs.

"That's right," the voice said.

Jack swung round. Staring straight at him was one of the most beautiful women he'd ever seen. She was dressed in a black sleeveless wetsuit and had long jet-black hair. Her hands were positioned behind her back. Covering both of her upper arms were detailed tattoos of Komodo dragons linked together by their tails. Standing behind her were two beefy male pirates, with torn shirts and equally detailed tattoos of the giant lizards on their arms.

For a moment, Jack couldn't take his eyes off of her. He couldn't believe she was on this ship with these terrible

pirates. Perhaps she, like Alfie, had been kidnapped and was here with them against her will.

"We *will* kill you," she added.

That comment shocked Jack out of his daydream.

"You shouldn't have come onto this ship," she said, her green eyes glaring at Jack. "Now, you're going to have to pay the price."

Jack panicked. How foolish he'd been in his rush to save Alfie! He should have known there might be a camera in this room. That's why no one was bothering to guard Alfie – they were probably watching him from that shack on the beach. This woman wasn't an innocent victim after all. She was the Komodo Klan's secret boss, and she was about to kill them both!

Jack watched in horror as she lifted an enormous spear gun from behind her back. At its tip was a dangerous-looking arrow, dripping with green goo. Before Jack could do anything, she lifted it straight at Jack and, without hesitation, pulled the trigger. A deadly spear flew into Jack's leg.

"Argh!" Jack screamed, clutching his leg. Despite the thickness of his wetsuit, the arrow still managed to pierce his skin. Blood began to ooze from his wound.

"That will teach you to come on board our ship and try to steal what is ours," she said, lowering her gun.

Within moments, the goo released a poison that was soon spreading through Jack's veins. His head felt fuzzy and his body went weak. He dropped to the floor, unable to stand, and then fell onto his forehead as if he were dead.

Chapter 11:
The Dragon

When Jack woke up, he was trapped
inside a small prison cell on top of the
boat. Although the bleeding for the most
part had stopped, his leg was still
throbbing with pain. He looked at his
Watch Phone. It was 1:30 PM. Just thirty
minutes after he'd been downstairs with
Alfie. As he panicked, a thought came to
him. Alfie! What had they done with him?

Just then a loud clanking noise came
from behind. Jack spun round. Opposite
him was another cage and inside was a

real Komodo dragon. Here he was, staring at the world's largest predatory lizard.

He knew two things about Komodo dragons. One, they were meat-eaters and not picky ones at that. They could bring down deer, wild boars, and even humans. Two, they killed their prey in two easy steps. They bit into it first, injecting deadly bacteria that paralysed their victims, then they returned later to finish them off.

"Well, I see you're awake," said a woman's voice from the other side. Jack whipped round. The boss lady was back.

"Glad to see the tranquillizer gun didn't stun you too much," she said as she flexed her arms. "I would have hated for you to be helpless. Woody here," she added, pointing to the dragon, "likes a challenge when it comes to eating his dinner."

Jack gulped. He reached for his Book Bag, but it was no longer there. In an instant, he panicked.

"If you're looking for your bag," she said, smiling smugly, "it's over there. We tried to open it, but the lock is a bit stubborn. Don't worry, in time we will crack it open, and everything inside will become a part of our collection."

Jack couldn't believe this was happening. Not only had he failed in his

attempt to rescue Alfie, but the GPF's
Secret Agent Book Bag was now in the
hands of pirates! How was he going to get
himself out of this situation?

"I'll check on you in a little while," the
woman said, turning away from Jack.

"What about Alfie?" said Jack, calling
over to her. "Where is he?"

"Now don't worry about that," she said,
looking back at Jack. "He's in a safe
place. We have plans
for him, too."

Jack watched as she signalled to a
male pirate, and the two of them
walked down the ramp and off the boat.
Jack looked over at Woody, whose two-
pronged tongue was slithering in and out

of his mouth. He grabbed the iron bars and shook them hard, hoping by some miracle they would rattle free. But they stood unshakable, trapping him inside. Jack thought about Max and wondered whether he'd ever been without a way out. He closed his eyes and thought of Max and quietly asked his brother to send him an answer.

Chapter 12:
The Break

Just then, he remembered Max telling him
about a mission he'd been on where his
opponent had trapped him inside a steel
storage locker. The only thing Max had
was his Watch Phone. Using the Melting
Ink Pen hidden inside, he was able to
draw a circle on the door and wait while
the inky chemical ate a hole through it.
Then Max was able to climb out and catch
the bad guy. Jack wondered if his Melting
Ink Pen would work on the thick iron bars
of the cage.

He lifted his Watch Phone towards his face and pushed the button on its right side. Instantly, a slim piece of aluminium ejected itself. He pulled it out and stretched it lengthwise. He twisted its top until the ink was at its tip and then rubbed it onto the bottom of one of the bars. Jack watched excitedly as the chemical popped and sizzled and within moments had cut through the iron. He did the same at the top, so that when he was finished he could pull the bar down and out of the way.

Thanks, Max, he said silently to his brother as he squeezed his body through the open space and ran for his Book Bag. He flung it over his shoulders and pulled his straps on tight.

"I'm not losing you again," said Jack, happy to have his protection back.

He dropped to his knees and peered out over the edge of the boat and across to the cay. The pirates were working hard and the boss lady was barking commands.

But where was Alfie? He put his Google Goggles back on and changed the setting to x-ray mode, then focused on the shack on the beach. Sure enough, Alfie was inside. This time he was guarded by a pirate with a rifle in his hands.

Jack needed to get to Alfie as soon as possible. But there was no way he could run onto the cay without being noticed. There were no bushes, no trees, and nowhere to hide. The only way he could rescue Alfie was to do it undercover and that meant he needed to vanish.

Slowly, he pulled the Disappearing Milk out of his bag and uncorked the bottle. He sighed, knowing that this would be the only time he'd ever get to use it. The GPF's Disappearing Milk was in short supply, and every secret agent only received one dose in his lifetime. Knowing its effects would last only ten minutes but that there wasn't another choice, he carefully poured half its contents over his head.

As it ran over his shoulders and down the length of his body, it began to make Jack's body disappear.

He looked at himself and when he was satisfied he couldn't see a thing, he dashed off the boat and down onto the beach.

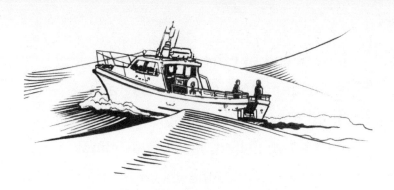

Chapter 13:
The Bold Escape

Up ahead, two pirates were wheeling boxes across the sand. Jack skirted round them and through the shack's front door. Inside the shack, Alfie was quietly dozing in his chair while the armed guard sat next to him, staring in the opposite direction.

Jack quietly reached into his Book Bag and pulled out his Dozing Spray. He walked over to the pirate and lifted his hand. He sprayed the fine mist into the pirate's nostrils and watched as he smiled and fell quickly to sleep.

Jack pulled out the rest of the Disappearing Milk from his bag and poured it over Alfie's head. When Alfie's body had vanished, Jack gently shook him until he woke up. Alfie was a bit shocked to open his eyes and find his body missing, but Jack whispered in his ear and told him everything was going to be all right.

The two of them dashed out of the hut. Unfortunately, the pirates' boss was walking through the front door at the same time. As they brushed by her, she stopped and tilted her head to one side. Then she looked across to the chair. When she realized that Alfie was missing, she sent one of the biggest human alarm calls Jack had ever heard.

"Komodos!" she yelled. "Someone has taken our prisoner!" She turned and looked out at the footprints the two boys were leaving in the sand. "And they're headed towards the ship!" she added. "Get them!"

Jack and Alfie were sprinting as fast as they could. As they were moving, Jack looked over his shoulder. Behind them were ten angry pirates with knives in their mouths and guns in their hands. As Jack was watching, one of them lifted his rifle and pulled the trigger.

"Watch out!" screamed Jack as he pulled

Alfie down and out of the way. A high-powered bullet shot through the air towards the two boys. They collapsed in the sand just as the bullet sailed over their heads.

"Get up!" Jack yanked Alfie to his feet. "Zigzag!" he yelled, running from side to side. Jack wanted to confuse the pirates by having their footprints dance around in the sand.

Jack and Alfie rushed towards the

pirate's ship and up the ramp. As soon they were on board, Jack grabbed the wheel that controlled the rope for the ramp and started turning it. With Alfie's help, the rope soon lifted the platform off the beach before any of the pirates could jump on. Instead they splashed into the water and fell face first into the sea.

When the rope was secure, Jack turned to Alfie. Both of their bodies were starting

to appear again. "Do you know how to sail this thing?" Jack asked.

"I think so," said Alfie, nodding and dashing towards the giant steering wheel in the middle of the boat.

As Alfie surveyed the wheel, Jack ran to the side of the boat. He looked down at shallow water around the cay. Some of the pirates and the boss lady were standing there, shaking their knuckled fists and yelling harsh words. Others were trudging through the water, trying to clamber up the slippery sides of the boat before falling back down. The pirate with the gun was still shooting bullets at them, but there was no way they could hit Jack and Alfie from where they were standing.

"Jack!" Alfie called. "I'm going to start her up! Can you lift the anchor so that we can get moving?"

"Yes, Captain!" said Jack.

He ran over to another wheel that held the anchor chain in place. With all his might, he pushed and then pulled on the handle, causing the wheel to turn. The anchor came away from the seabed. As Alfie started the engines, the boat began to move away from the cay. When they were far enough away from the pirates and their weapons, Jack returned to Alfie.

"How are we doing?" he asked, placing a hand on Alfie's shoulder.

"Great," said Alfie. "I have us headed

 for the *Explorer*. We should be there in no time."

Chapter 14:
The Noise

Ah, freedom, thought Jack. He breathed a sigh of relief. They had escaped the clutches of the pirates and were on their way to safety. Jack looked towards the back of the boat and spied the box with the name *PANDORA* written on it. He had successfully rescued Alfie, captured the pirate ship, and saved the stolen treasure. The pirates were trapped on the island with nowhere to go. Jack figured he and Alfie had a few minutes to relax.

"Do you want something to drink?" he asked Alfie.

"Sure would," said Alfie, equally relieved to be off the cay.

Jack walked over to the hole in the deck and lowered himself down. He opened one of the cupboards and found a hidden fridge behind the door. Inside were two extremely cold-looking bottles of water. He grabbed them and closed the door with his foot.

Just then, Jack heard a strange noise. *THUD!* It was coming from upstairs. It sounded as if something had landed on the deck above his head.

THUD! There it was again.

"Alfie?" Jack yelled upstairs, waiting for a response. But none came.

Jack put down the bottles. Slowly he climbed the stairs and poked his head out of the hole. He looked at the wheel where Alfie had been standing, but there was no one there. The boat seemed to be sailing itself.

"Alfie?" Jack said again, this time a bit more quietly. "Are you all right?"

"Don't move," said a female voice from behind Jack's head. His heart started beating loudly as he turned round and found himself staring, once again, down the shaft of a long, familiar spear.

Chapter 15:
The Push

"You're clever, but not as clever as I am.
Now get up!" the boss lady hissed.
Another pirate was standing behind her
with an evil grin on his face.

Jack was confused. He'd watched the
pirates disappear as he and Alfie sailed
away.

"In case you were wondering how we
managed to board," she said, almost
reading Jack's mind, "let's just say, you're
not the only one with gadgets." She
yanked Jack up to the main deck.

As he fell onto the deck, Jack noticed
two Human Helicopters lying on their
sides. Max had told him about these
criminal gadgets, which enabled crooks to
fly short distances. That must have been
how they arrived on the boat.

Just then, Jack heard a clanking sound
from Woody, the Komodo dragon. The
other pirate was holding Alfie in front of
its cage.

"Now," she said to Jack, keeping the
spear pointed at his face. "I told you
before you should not have come on this

ship. This is our business, and I don't appreciate a little runt like you coming along and messing things up. This is the last time you and your friend come between me and my treasure."

"Jake!" she yelled over to the pirate holding Alfie. "Introduce him to Woody. And as for this one" – she leaned close to Jack and looked at him with her emerald-colored eyes – "I will have the pleasure of escorting him off the ship and to his death."

Before Jack could react, the pirate

guarding Alfie opened the Komodo's cage and swiftly tossed Alfie inside. The dragon let its forked tongue slither out before it leaped forwards to bite Alfie's right arm. Alfie

screamed in agony, and then fainted on the spot.

"Alfie!" screamed Jack, trying to rouse him. But there was nothing Jack could do. The Komodo had inflicted its deadly bacteria. Now it would leave Alfie alone while it took effect. Jack, meanwhile, had problems of his own.

"Well," said the boss lady, "that should

be the end of him." She glared at Jack. "Now, why don't we introduce you to the dangers of swimming in the waters of the reef?"

Continuing to point her spear gun, she motioned for Jack to walk to the other side of the boat where a plank was being lowered over the ocean.

"If my timing is right," she said, "the jellies will have been swept into these waters. I'm sure they would love to meet you."

Jack knew that jellyfish, not sharks, were among the most deadly predators living in the Great Barrier Reef. The Irukandji jellyfish, in particular, was so deadly that a sting from one of them could kill you in as little as five minutes.

As Jack was shoved onto the plank and towards its end, he looked down at the ocean. It seemed as if hundreds of

Irukandji jellyfish were directly under the plank, each one with four deadly tentacles hanging from its bell-shaped body.

Jack closed his eyes. He had to figure out a way to escape from this situation. While he was desperately formulating his plan, the force of the boss lady's foot hit him in the back. He yelled out as she sent him toppling over the end of the plank and towards the ferocious waters that lay below.

Chapter 16:
The Jellies

Before he'd been pushed over the edge,
several thoughts had run through Jack's
mind. The first was that Irukandji jellyfish
were known to exist only at the surface
of the water. The second was that his
Oxygen Exchanger was inside his Book
Bag. This meant that, even though Jack
held the record for holding his breath
underwater at the Surrey Sharks' training
pool, he probably only had twenty
seconds to recover from the fall, open his
bag, and get it out. The last was that three

parts of his body were exposed to the sting of the Irukandji jellyfish – his hands, his face and his feet.

After he was pushed, Jack tried to remember what he'd been taught about diving off a board. As soon as he was in the air, he took a deep breath and positioned himself so that his arms were covering his face and his hands were pointed as narrowly as possible when he hit the water face first.

SPLASH!

Jack entered the sea with a thunderous roar. The momentum from the fall sent him pummelling through the water like a torpedo. Keeping his eyes closed, he counted to himself, guessing how many feet he had dived. One . . . two . . . three . . .

When he reached fifteen feet, he slowed his body down. He opened his eyes and

then closed them again in relief. At that depth, he figured the jellyfish would be gone. He was right. He was surrounded on all sides by nothing but clear, blue water. And because he had dived with such speed, the jellyfish hadn't had time to sting. But the cut on his leg was stinging instead, as the salty seawater began to seep through the arrow hole in his wetsuit.

The pressure in his lungs from holding his breath was building up. He needed to get to his Oxygen Exchanger, and fast. He reached into his bag and pulled it out. As quickly as he could, he placed it in his mouth and wrapped the tubes around his head. He took lots of deep breaths – with fresh oxygen in his body he could now figure out what to do.

He strapped his Google Goggles back on and looked at the swarming mass of jellyfish above. There was no way he could swim into that. The only way Jack was going to be able to rise to the surface was to find a break in the jellies.

He twisted the rims on his goggles and looked into the distance. To his right, he noticed some light beaming down through the sea. Figuring it was a hole, Jack started to swim.

But as he was swimming, something barrelled into his back. It tossed him forwards and pushed the breath from his lungs. He sucked on his mouthpiece to regain his breath and shook his head. Surely the boss lady wasn't down here kicking him again!

THUD!

This time it hit him from the side, sending him sideways in the water. As Jack tried to figure out what had actually hit him, a dark grey figure swam before his eyes. Almost immediately Jack recognized its shape. It was one of the most common predators of the Great Barrier Reef – the grey reef shark. And, unfortunately for Jack, there wasn't just one. There were two.

Chapter 17:
The Sharks

Sensing they were about to attack, Jack slowly reached into his Book Bag and pulled out the Spray Gun. Keeping an eye on the sharks, he flicked open his Vial Box and took out the tube marked *B* for *blood*. He inserted it into the barrel of the Spray Gun and then pulled the trigger as hard as he could. The tube with the blood shot through the water and exploded in the distance, far away from Jack.

Almost as soon as it burst, the sharks started to swim away. Jack knew the scent of blood would attract them towards it. For now at least, he had some time. He turned in the direction of the hole and started swimming again.

When he finally reached the hole he put his head above the water. He lifted his hands to his goggles and twisted the rims. Already, the Komodo Klan's pirate ship was at least a mile away. He lifted his hand and pushed a button on his Watch Phone. Within minutes, The Egg appeared, just below his feet.

It drifted up to Jack and opened its hatch. Jack swam inside and closed the hatch, then activated the pump. Immediately, the water that had been inside was forced out through a hole, and soon Jack was able to take off his Oxygen Exchanger.

He turned his attention to the dashboard and punched in the coordinates of his destination. As The Egg began to move, Jack thought about the situation ahead. The boss lady had got the better of him, not once, but twice. He *had* to capture her, save Alfie, and rescue the treasure this time around or he'd feel like a failure. As The Egg cruised through the waters of the reef, he planned his final strike.

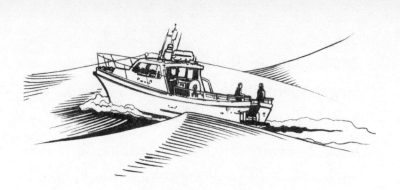

Chapter 18:
The Last Try

When The Egg drifted alongside the
pirate's ship, Jack instructed it to surface
and pop its hatch. But this time there was
no anchor chain on the side of the boat
for him to climb, so he punched the *lift*
feature on his chair. Slowly, it lifted itself
upwards so that Jack was positioned near
the top of the boat. Carefully, he looked
across the deck.

As far as he could tell, both the boss
lady and her pirate assistant, Jake, were
nowhere in sight. Jack twisted his Google

Goggles to the *x-ray* setting and found them below, sitting at a table and looking at a map. They hadn't wasted any time planning their escape.

He looked over at Alfie, who was completely dazed. Jack climbed over the rail and onto the deck, then raced across it towards Woody's cage. He yanked open the door, grabbing Alfie, and pulled him to safety just as the Komodo dragon leaped and tried to bite them both.

But Alfie wasn't moving. Jack put his ear to Alfie's mouth and listened for breathing. It was light, but there was a faint hint of a breath. He was still alive!

Quickly, Jack opened his Vial Box and pulled out the tube marked *A*. He loaded the antibiotic, switched the gun's setting to *syringe* and injected the medicine into Alfie's arm. He then pulled out

some gauze and wrapped it around Alfie's arm.

"That should help," Jack whispered in his ear.

Just then, Jack heard a commotion under his feet. It was the boss lady and she was climbing the stairs. This was the moment Jack had been waiting for. He left Alfie lying on the deck and ran for the bottom rung of a climbing net that stretched to the top of the middle mast. He climbed the net, one rung at a time, until he reached the top.

"Finally," he said to himself, "a chance to teach this dragon lady a lesson." He loaded the Spray Gun with a new tube marked *T* returned the setting to *spray*, and waited.

Chapter 19:
The Stand-Off

Almost as soon as the boss lady emerged, she noticed that Alfie had been moved from his cage. She pulled her spear gun from behind her back and began to creep around.

"Seems we have a visitor," she said out loud to Jake. "I wonder if that boy has foolishly come back."

"Sure have!" Jack shouted from his position on the mast.

In response, the boss lady whipped around and looked up at Jack. Because

Jack had cleverly positioned himself in line with the sun, it was difficult for her to see. She strained her eyes to focus, raised her spear gun, and pulled the trigger. A spear shot through the air towards Jack, but he simply ducked and it flew over his head.

She growled to herself. "I've got plenty more where that came from!" she yelled, pulling another spear from behind her back. She placed it at the tip of the gun and smiled viciously.

"I've got something for you too!" replied Jack, as he pulled *his* weapon from behind *his* back. He lifted the Spray Gun and pointed it directly at her.

"You wouldn't dare!" she grizzled.

"Oh, yes, I would," said Jack, beaming as he pulled the trigger. The boss lady dived to the right, trying to avoid the vial. But it caught her on her tattooed arm and burst all over her.

"Nooooo!" she screamed as her speech began to slur. Desperate, she tried to lift her gun, but it was too heavy. She collapsed on the deck, dropping her weapon. Then she fell fast asleep as the tranquillizing liquid took effect.

"You little brat!" yelled Jake, seeing his boss sprawled on the floor. He ran for a rifle that was lying on a box near the side of the boat, but Jack sent a tranquillizing vial his way too. It exploded all over his chest and within moments he, too, was knocked out.

Jack was ecstatic. He scurried down the net and onto the deck. He reached into his Book Bag and pulled out two pairs of handcuffs, then he cuffed the two evil villains to a metal rail.

"That should keep you until the authorities arrive," he said.

Now that the danger was over, Jack ran across to Alfie. The powerful antibiotic that Jack had injected seemed to be working. Alfie was finally starting to wake up.

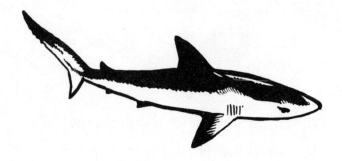

Chapter 20:
The Treasure

Jack lifted his Watch Phone and called the Australian Water Police. He told them what had happened and asked them to come and take the pirates away. He then called Harry, who had been patiently waiting on the *Explorer* for any news.

"Hi, Harry," said Jack when he got through.

"Well, I'll be!" said Harry. "I hope this is good news."

"Sure is," said Jack. "Want to come onboard?"

"Would love to," said Harry. Jack could tell he was pleased. "I've never been on a real pirate ship before."

Within the hour, both the Water Police and Harry arrived. As the authorities were dragging the boss lady and her henchman away, their doctor was tending to Alfie's

wounds. Another squad of police were heading off for the pirates on the cay. No doubt they'd be spending a lifetime in jail. Jack knew the fines for stealing shipwreck treasures were steep, especially in Australia.

"Come with me," said Jack, leading Harry to the back of the boat. He showed him the box with the word PANDORA.

"Well, well," said Harry, his eyes opening wide. "Is this what they took from the wreck below?"

"Yep," said Jack. "Shall we open it together?"

The two of them lifted the top of the box and peered inside. There amidst some packing paper was a black rectangular box with gold-painted decorations. It looked as if it had come all the way from Asia. Harry gently reached in and lifted it out. He opened the tiny latch that held it together and gasped.

Piled high inside were what looked like hundreds of gold coins, twinkling and glimmering in the afternoon sun. Nestled among the coins were all sorts of jewels, including sapphires, emeralds, and

green-colored jade. From the look of it, Jack figured the loot was worth millions of dollars.

"Well," said Jack, happy he was able to give this to Harry, "I think my time here is just about up."

"I can't thank you enough," said Harry, still stunned by the find. "The museum and I are truly grateful." He nodded towards Alfie, who was still a bit woozy. "And I'm sure Alfie would thank you too if he could."

"No worries," said Jack. "It's part of my job."

He looked at his Watch Phone. It was time to go. He waved to Harry and then made his way across the deck of the ship. He climbed over the edge and into The Egg's chair. Sensing he was in position, the chair began to lower itself down.

Once he was inside the boat, the arched door came over and sealed him inside. He punched a few buttons and a map of the United Kingdom appeared on the dash. After marking his coordinates, he pushed the *submerge* button. Slowly The Egg lowered itself into the waters of the reef.

From inside the map, a tiny light began to glow. It grew in brilliance until it had filled the entire pod. When he was ready, Jack yelled, "Off to England!" Then the light flickered and burst, swallowing him whole and transporting him home.

The Mystery
of the
Mona Lisa:
FRANCE

BOOK ③

The Mystery of the Mona Lisa: FRANCE

Elizabeth Singer Hunt

Illustrated by Brian Williamson

WEINSTEIN
BOOKS

ISBN: 1-60286-001-7
ISBN 13: 978-1-60286-001-8

First Edition
10   9   8   7   6   5

For Andy, Morgan, and Corinne

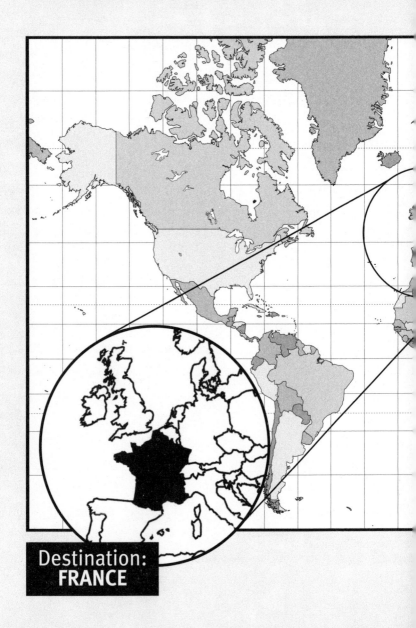

Destination:
FRANCE

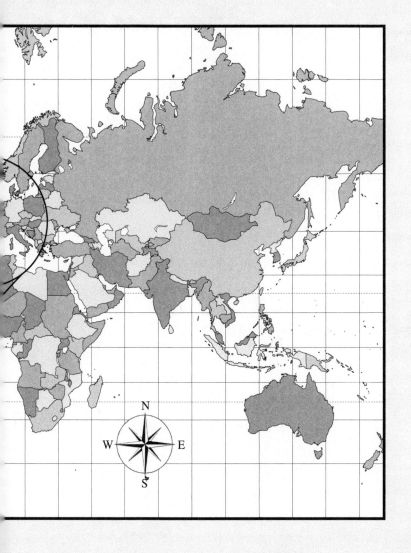

My name is Jack Stalwart. My older brother,

Max, was a secret agent for you, until he

disappeared on one of your missions. Now I

want to be a secret agent, too. If you choose

me, I will be an excellent secret agent and get

rid of evil villains, just like my brother did.

Sincerely,

Jack Stalwart

HIGHLY CONFIDENTIAL

Jack Stalwart was sworn in as a Global Protection Force secret agent four months ago. Since that time, he has completed all of his missions successfully and has stopped no less than twelve evil villains. Because of this he has been assigned the code name COURAGE.

Jack has yet to uncover the whereabouts of his brother, Max, who is still working for this organization at a secret location. Do not give Secret Agent Jack Stalwart this information. He is never to know about his brother.

Gerald Barter

Gerald Barter
Director, Global Protection Force

THINGS YOU'LL FIND IN EVERY BOOK

 **Watch Phone:** The only gadget Jack wears all the time, even when he's not on official business. His Watch Phone is the central gadget that makes most others work. There are lots of important features, most importantly the C button, which reveals the code of the day – necessary to unlock Jack's Secret Agent Book Bag. There are buttons on both sides, one of which ejects his life-saving Melting Ink Pen. Beyond these functions, it also works as a phone and, of course, gives Jack the time of day.

 **Global Protection Force (GPF):** The GPF is the organization Jack works for. It's a worldwide force of young secret agents whose aim is to protect the world's people, places, and possessions. No one knows exactly where its main offices are located (all correspondence and gadgets for repair are sent to a special PO Box, and training is held at various locations around the world), but Jack thinks it's somewhere cold, like the Arctic Circle.

Whizzy: Jack's magical miniature globe. Almost every night at precisely 7:30 PM, the GPF uses Whizzy to send Jack the identity of the country that he must travel to. Whizzy can't talk, but he can cough up messages. Jack's parents don't know Whizzy is anything more than a normal globe.

The Magic Map: The magical map hanging on Jack's bedroom wall. Unlike most maps, the GPF's map is made of a mysterious wood. Once Jack inserts the country piece from Whizzy, the map swallows Jack whole and sends him away on his missions. When he returns, he arrives precisely one minute after he left.

Secret Agent Book Bag: The Book Bag that Jack wears on every adventure. Licensed only to GPF secret agents, it contains top-secret gadgets necessary to foil bad guys and escape certain death. To activate the bag before each mission, Jack must punch in a secret code given to him by his Watch Phone. Once he's away, all he has to do is place his finger on the zipper, which identifies him as the owner of the bag and immediately opens.

THE STALWART FAMILY

Jack's dad, John

He moved the family to England when Jack was two, in order to take a job with an aerospace company. As far as Jack knows, his dad designs and manufactures aeroplane parts. Jack's dad thinks he is an ordinary boy and that his other son, Max, attends a school in Switzerland. Jack's dad is American and his mum is British, which makes Jack a bit of both.

Jack's mum, Corinne

One of the greatest mums as far as Jack is concerned. When she and her husband received a letter from a posh school in Switzerland inviting Max to attend, they were overjoyed. Since Max left six months ago, they have received numerous notes in Max's handwriting telling them he's OK. Little do they know it's all a lie and that it's the GPF sending those letters.

Jack's older brother, Max

Two years ago, at the age of nine, Max joined the GPF. Max used to tell Jack about his adventures and show him how to work his secret-agent gadgets. When the family received a letter inviting Max to attend a school in Europe, Jack figured it was to do with the GPF. Max told him he was right, but that he couldn't tell Jack anything about why he was going away.

Nine-year-old Jack Stalwart

Four months ago, Jack received an anonymous note saying: "Your brother is in danger. Only you can save him." As soon as he could, Jack applied to be a secret agent, too. Since that time, he's battled some of the world's most dangerous villains and hopes some day in his travels to find and rescue Max.

DESTINATION:
France

France is located on the continent of Europe.

◻

Paris is the capital city of France.

◻

Almost nine million people live in this city.

◻

One of the world's most famous museums, the Louvre, is located in Paris.

◻

France is a member of the European Union and its currency is the euro.

French people love eating interesting food, including snails, which are called *escargot* (pronounced *s-car-go*) in French.

◻

The Eiffel Tower, one of the most famous landmarks in Paris, is over a thousand feet high and was the tallest structure in the world until 1931.

◻

The English Channel is a narrow sea that separates the north of France from England.

The Great Travel Guide

SECRET AGENT PHRASEBOOK
FOR FRANCE

MONA LISA:
Facts and Figures

The *Mona Lisa* was painted by Leonardo da Vinci and is one of the most famous paintings in the world.

□

It was probably painted between 1503 and 1506.

□

Originally the painting was larger than today, but at some point the sides were cut off.

□

Each year millions of people visit the Louvre museum in Paris where is it on display.

On Monday, August 21, 1911, the *Mona Lisa* was actually stolen from the Louvre by a man named Vincenzo Perugia. It took the police over two years to find it.

□

The painting measures just about 21 x 30 inches and is hung behind unbreakable glass to protect it.

PLACES IN PARIS

Arc de Triomphe (pronounced *Ark da Tree-omf*)

Champs Elysées (pronounced *Shoms El-ee-zay*)

The Eiffel Tower (pronounced *I-fill*)

Musée du Louvre (pronounced *Mew-say do Loo-vre*)

Musée de l'Homme (pronounced *Mew-say de lom*)

Musée d'Orsay (pronounced *Mew-say Dor-say*)

Place de la Concorde
(pronounced *Plass de la Con-cord*)

Pompidou (pronounced *Pom-pee-do*)

River Seine (pronounced *Sane*)

Tuileries Gardens (pronounced *Too-i-ler-ee*)

SECRET AGENT GADGET INSTRUCTION MANUAL

Magic Key Maker: One of the most useful gadgets in the GPF arsenal. It's perfect when you don't have a key to open a lock. Just insert this long, rubber stick into a keyhole or ignition and watch as it melts and oozes inside. Wait a few seconds for it to harden into a key and then use it to gain access to whatever you need.

Time-Release Vapors:

Whenever another secret agent or trusted contact has been knocked out, use the Time-Release Vapors to restore to consciousness. Just open the tub, place a small amount of the cream on your finger and rub it under the agent's nose. The vapors should work within minutes.

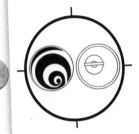

The Hypno-Disk: One of the most useful gadgets available to GPF secret agents today. The Hypno-Disk has two functions: 1) to hypnotize your opponent and 2) to save you from deadly force fields (lasers, hypnotizing lights, etc.). To activate, turn the dial on the back of this circular disk in a clockwise direction. The disk will spin, throwing out a hypnotic light that will transfix your opponent. To save yourself from force fields coming your way, turn the dial on the back in a counter-clockwise direction. The spinning will reverse, sucking any deadly light into the device and trapping it there.

Chapter 1:
The Vanishing Lady

The museum in Paris had been closed for several hours and the Bon Homme cleaning crew were busy at work. Over a hundred cleaners were scurrying through the huge museum, mopping the floors and dusting the railings, taking care not to damage the precious paintings that hung on the walls.

One of the rooms in the museum is known as the *"Mona Lisa* Room," because on a special fake wall in the middle hangs the most famous painting in the world.

The *Mona Lisa* is a painting of a woman clothed in a brown dress with a mysterious smile on her face. It was painted over four hundred years ago by an artist named Leonardo da Vinci. It is so valuable that the museum has invested in a bullet-proof-glass security box, which is fixed over the painting to protect it from anyone who wants to do it harm.

On this night, Hélène, one of Bon Homme's senior cleaners, made her way to the *Mona Lisa* room. As usual, she entered the room after her assistant, Jean Paul, had mopped the floor. She walked over to the glass box with the *Mona Lisa* inside and pulled out a special dusting cloth. She lifted the cloth and tried to wipe over it. But something was wrong. The front of the box was no longer there.

Hélène blinked twice and then let out a

piercing scream that shook the entire room. "The *Mona Lisa* is gone!" she screamed. "The world's most famous painting has been stolen from the Louvre!"

Chapter 2:
The Magic Map

In a different country, nine-year-old Secret
Agent Jack Stalwart was sitting in his
bedroom at his desk doing his homework.
His fourth grade art teacher, Mr. Yates,
had asked the students to draw a picture
of their favorite comic-book hero by the
next day. Jack's choice, Super Smash, was
one of four superheroes who lived on the
planet Green and battled with the likes
of Tortua, the nastiest female villain ever
seen. Jack loved reading about Super
Smash's adventures and was thinking

about doing just that when there was a
knock from inside his right-hand desk
drawer.

Drat, thought Jack. He knew what that
meant. He looked at his Watch Phone.
It was 7:00 PM. He carefully opened the
drawer and peeked inside. There, lying in
his desk, was a new DVD. The GPF often
snuck
things
like
that
into Jack's
room as a way
to prepare him for his upcoming
missions. This DVD was entitled: *Da
Vinci's Masterpiece: The Mona Lisa*.

He carried it over to the TV in the
corner of his room and put it into the
built-in DVD player. Almost instantly, a
program on the history of the famous

painting began. What Jack didn't know, the DVD told him, so that by the time it was finished he was fully informed. He looked at his Watch Phone as the credits rolled. It was 7:30 PM.

Just as he expected, a familiar whirring sound came from the other corner of his room. His trusty miniature globe, Whizzy, was starting to spin. Jack rushed over to Whizzy. By now the globe was spinning so hard that he had smoke coming out of his ears.

"Come on, Whizzy!" Jack cheered. "I know you can do it."

"Ahem!" coughed Whizzy, and out of his mouth popped a jigsaw piece in the

shape of an unknown country. It landed on the floor next to Jack's foot. Whizzy let out a big whoosh as he settled down again.

"This one is quite large," commented Jack as he picked up the piece. "And after seeing that DVD, I bet I know where I'm going tonight."

Jack carried the piece over to the far side of his bedroom, to the large map of the world that was hanging on his wall. It looked just like an ordinary map, but in fact it was a Magic Map from the GPF. It transported him around the world to battle evil villains and bring them to justice.

He lifted the piece and placed it over the map. He steered it towards the center of Europe and instantly the jigsaw slotted in. Jack stepped back to take a look. The name FRANCE appeared, then quickly vanished.

"France!" said Jack. "I knew it had to be France! I can't wait to go."

Jack tapped the C button on his Watch Phone. Instantly the code of the day was displayed across its screen. He dashed over to his bed and knelt down next to it, pulling his Book Bag out from underneath. He punched in the code on its lock – C-H-E-E-S-E – and unzipped the bag, looking inside. He had to make sure that all of his secret-agent gadgets were there before he left.

Magic Key Maker. Check. Magic Steps. Check. Melting Ink Pen. Check. Jack closed the bag and turned to Whizzy. "I think I'm ready to go," he said.

Jack raced back to the wall just as a warm yellow light was beginning to glow inside the country of France. The beam continued to grow until Jack's room was filled with brightness.

"Off to France!" Jack cried. And with those words, the yellow light burst and swallowed Jack into the Magic Map.

Chapter 3:
The Glass Museum

When Jack arrived he noticed two things. The first was that it was morning and the second was that he was standing in the middle of a large pyramid with a glass ceiling. For a moment he wondered whether the map had thrown him off course.

"Am I in Egypt?" he wondered out loud.

"No. I can assure you that you are not in Egypt," a voice said from behind. "You are in Paris, the capital city of France. I am Chief Inspector Henri Pierre. You must be

Jack," he said, extending his hand. "The Global Protection Force said that it would be sending the finest."

Chief Inspector Henri Pierre was a large man with a big belly, who looked as if he had enjoyed too many puddings. When he smiled his eyes twinkled and his moustache wriggled. Although Henri Pierre was losing his hair, he still looked very young to be a chief inspector.

"Nice to meet you, Chief Inspector," said Jack, showing his GPF badge.

"You can call me Henri," said the chief
inspector.

"Well then, Henri, what seems to be the
problem?" Jack asked, eager to find out
about his next mission.

"You are standing in the middle of the
Louvre, one of the world's greatest
museums," explained Henri. "Inside here
are some of the rarest and most

expensive pieces of art. Last night, one of our most precious paintings, the *Mona Lisa*, was stolen right from under our noses. We think it happened sometime between closing time at 6:00 PM, and 8:00 PM, when one of the cleaners noticed that it was missing."

"I don't understand," said Jack. "Didn't your video surveillance equipment record the thief in action?"

"No, it didn't," answered Henri. "It is most strange – there is no record of anyone going in or out of the room before the cleaners," he added. "That is why we called the GPF. We need your special skills to find the *Mona Lisa* and make sense of this horrible mess."

"No problem, Henri," said Jack. "I'm sure I can find the *Mona Lisa* and return it to the museum. First I'd like to see the room where the painting was stolen from. Then I'd like to meet the cleaner who discovered that it was missing. He or she might be able to provide some clues that could help in the investigation."

"I agree," said the chief inspector. "First things first," he went on. "Let me show you to the *Mona Lisa* room."

Chapter 4: The Investigation

Jack followed Henri through the halls of the museum past some of the most amazing works of art that Jack had ever seen. Beyond the *Mona Lisa* painting, Jack knew that the Louvre was famous for containing art from Ancient Egypt and Greece.

Mr. Yates often talked about the Louvre museum and even promised to take Jack's class on a field trip there one day. Jack passed through a room filled with sculptures of men, then came upon a room with a lone wall in the middle.

Henri pointed up ahead. "That's where the lady of the museum used to hang," he said, referring to the *Mona Lisa*. "You can see the thief was able not only to get past our security systems but also to cut off the front of the bullet-proof-glass box that helped protect her."

Jack walked over to the wall and looked up at what was left. There was a hook where the painting had hung and the remains of the outer box. What was strange to Jack was that whatever had sawn through the box had done it so that the cut was nice and flat. Normally, Jack reasoned, when glass was broken there were jags or breaks in the glass left behind. But when Jack ran his finger over its edge, the glass was perfectly smooth.

"The only thing I know that can cut this finely," said Jack to Henri, "is a laser."

"A laser, you say," said Henri, some-what surprised. "That's an interesting observation."

"And as far as I can tell there don't seem to be any pieces of laser equipment left behind," said Jack as he looked around the room. "What about fingerprints?" he continued, carrying on with questions related to his investigation.

"We've already dusted," said the chief inspector. "I sent a team in as soon as the *Mona Lisa* was discovered missing. They scoured the walls, railings and, of course, the glass box itself. When I got word that you were on your way, I told the team to clear out until you were finished. The only part of the room they didn't get to examine was the floor."

Jack got down on his hands and knees and looked across the floor of the great room for any clues. Just ahead of him, he spied a single strand of hair. It was such a distinctive shade of red, he couldn't help but notice it. He picked it up and examined it closely.

Knowing that Inspector Pierre's team had been all over the place dusting for fingerprints, he turned to Henri.

"Does anyone in your team have red hair like this one?" he asked, showing the strand to Henri. He was trying to eliminate one of the chief inspector's officers as the one who'd left the hair.

"No," replied Henri. "No one has red hair like that."

Given what Henri had just said, Jack figured it had been left by either the last cleaner to leave the room or by the crook.

Jack crouched down to his knees and opened his Book Bag. Inside was a clear, square box with a silver digital display on

the outside. This was the GPF's DNA Decoder. Since everyone in the world has a different DNA — or part of the cells that tells our bodies what to do and what to look like — the GPF developed the DNA Decoder. It could take something as simple as a hair and tell a secret agent who it belonged to.

"Do you mind if I analyze this?" asked Jack, referring to the strand of hair.

"Not at all," said the chief inspector. "Be my guest."

Jack took the DNA Decoder out and opened it up, placing the single strand of hair inside. He closed it and pushed the DECODE button. Instantly the results were displayed: UNKNOWN.

Great, thought Jack, shaking his head in frustration. If this were the hair of the crook, Jack figured he or she was a first-timer.

"Well," said Jack, standing up and gathering his evidence and his bag, "I think it's time I met the cleaner."

"Certainly," said Henri. "The person you need to speak to is Hélène. She's sitting downstairs waiting to be interviewed. I'll show you the way."

Chapter 5:
The Interview

Jack followed Henri down two floors to a
small room on the lower level. Waiting
for him was a woman with brown hair
dressed in a blue-and-white-striped
cleaner's uniform. She was sitting on a
chair beside a desk. As far as Jack could
tell she looked like an honest woman,
although Jack knew you could never be
sure. She seemed to be terribly upset by
the whole thing as she was crying a lot
and spent most of her time wiping the
tears away from her eyes.

"*Bonjour*," said Jack as he closed the

door behind him. *"Je m'appelle Jack Stalwart."*

"Hello," replied the woman. She could tell that Jack wasn't from France, so she spoke to him in English. "My name is Hélène," she said.

"I am here from the Global Protection Force," Jack explained. "I'm trying to figure out who took the *Mona Lisa*. As you know, this is a very serious crime and therefore everyone involved is a suspect."

Hélène wiped her tears away again and looked across at him with scared eyes.

"Can you tell me," he asked, "what you were doing when you noticed the painting was missing and exactly what you saw?"

Hélène thought for a moment. "Well," she said, "as I told Chief Inspector Pierre, I was on my way into the *Mona Lisa* room when my assistant, Jean Paul, rushed out.

I didn't think that much of it at the time, because Jean Paul is a bit of a nervous person. But then," she added, "I walked into the room and up to the box to clean the case and then I noticed it wasn't there."

"What wasn't there?" asked Jack, making sure he understood her story.

"The *Mona Lisa*," she said. "And the box, too. Well, at least the front of it."

"Did you touch anything?" he asked.

"No," she said. "I left immediately and reported the theft to security."

"What about Jean Paul?" said Jack. "Did he say anything to you?" By now, Jack was thinking that perhaps Jean Paul had something to do with the crime.

"Not a thing," she said, sniffing and wiping her eyes.

"What color hair does Jean Paul have?" asked Jack.

"Brown," said Hélène. "Although sometimes in the light," she added, "it can look a bit red."

Interesting, thought Jack as he and Henri looked at each other. He wondered if the hair he had found belonged to Jean Paul.

"It sounds as if I need to speak with Jean Paul," said Jack. He'd pretty much ruled out Hélène as a suspect. "Do you know where he lives?" he asked.

"He lives near the Eiffel Tower on Rue St Charles," offered Hélène. "In the house to the right of the barber shop."

"Thanks," said Jack. "In the meantime," he suggested, "call Chief Inspector Pierre if you think of anything else."

Hélène nodded and left the room, still sniffing back tears.

Jack rifled through his pocket and pulled out his secret-agent map of Paris. The Eiffel Tower and Rue St Charles weren't far from the Louvre.

"Rue St Charles, here I come," he said to himself as he walked towards the door. "Let's see if this Jean Paul can add anything else to the clues of this crime."

Chapter 6:
The Chase

When Jack walked out of the great doors of the Louvre, he found himself in the middle of a square with a giant fountain and lots of pretty flowers. In the distance, he could see people lounging in chairs near a water feature and a collection of beautiful trees and shrubs. He looked at his map. It looked as if he were facing a garden called the Tuileries.

He turned left through the Tuileries and headed towards a river called the Seine. The mighty Seine flowed right through the city of Paris, according to Jack's city map. He crossed over a bridge and turned right, following the Seine as it wound its way around. Up ahead he could see the Eiffel Tower, a massive iron monument that soars up into the sky and has an aerial on top that sends signals across the country.

Jack passed the Eiffel Tower and headed down Rue St. Charles. The barber shop Hélène mentioned was on the corner.

When he reached the house, he stopped and knocked on the door.

There was no answer. He knocked again, this time a bit harder.

"*Bonjour*," said a shy male voice from the other side.

"*Bonjour*," said Jack. "My name is Jack Stalwart and I am here to see Jean Paul. Is he in?"

All of a sudden Jack heard a clang and the sound of feet running away from the door. He heard a thud and then there was silence.

Jack called out. "Jean Paul, is that you? Are you OK?" Still there was no answer.

Quickly, Jack tried to open the door. He was in luck – it was unlocked. He stepped inside and looked around. From an open window to his right, he could hear footsteps running down the street. He dashed to the window and looked outside.

"Jean Paul!" Jack yelled to the man who was running away. From what Jack could see, the man had reddish-brown hair. "I just want to ask you a few questions!"

But the man kept running. Jack raced back to the front door and out onto the street, then started running in the same direction.

The man was running so fast and with such big strides, it was hard for Jack to keep up. He chased him as he raced past the Eiffel Tower and across a bridge. After that, the man headed towards the Place de la Concorde and turned right down a small road. He dashed past the post office, a supermarket, and a bakery and down another street to the right.

"Wait!" Jack gasped. "I just want to talk to you!"

Eventually the road that the man was running along ended and he was trapped with nowhere else to go. He turned to Jack with fear in his eyes.

"I didn't do it! I didn't do it!" he said, panting and trying to catch his breath.

"What do you mean?" asked Jack.

"I didn't steal the *Mona Lisa*," said the man.

"Then why are you running away if you didn't do it?" asked Jack, still blocking his way.

"Because I saw something," the man said, gasping for breath, "and I am afraid. I am afraid for my life."

Chapter 7:
The Confession

"It's OK," said Jack, trying to calm him down. "Maybe if you tell me what you saw I can help." Jack wasn't entirely sure whether to trust Jean Paul, but for the moment he figured he'd give him a chance to explain.

The man plonked himself down on a dirty bench next to a rubbish heap and slumped over with his face in his hands.

"My name *is* Jean Paul," he said, looking up at Jack. "I work for Bon Homme Cleaners. I am Hélène's assistant. We are in charge of the *Mona Lisa* room."

"Last night," explained Jean Paul, "after I'd finished mopping the other floors, I went back to the room to pick up a bucket I'd left behind. When I approached, I saw a man standing in front of the *Mona Lisa.* I crouched down and peered around the corner to get a good look.

"You see," Jean Paul added, "Hélène and I are the only ones allowed in the room after the museum closes and I thought it was strange that he was in there." He carried on, "He put a black glove on his right hand. Then, out of nowhere, five thin red lights shot from his fingertips! He moved his hand around the edges of the box that protected the *Mona Lisa* and the lights sliced the front off as if it were a soft cheese! I was so scared that I ran away, past Hélène and out of the museum." Jack thought Jean Paul's description was interesting, as he'd already guessed that it was a laser that had cut the glass. Maybe he was telling the truth.

"Why didn't you tell someone?" asked Jack.

"I was scared." Jean Paul sighed. "I thought no one would believe me. And even if they did, I didn't want

the person who did this to know I was
the one who saw him. He might come
after me."

"Can you tell me anything about the
man himself?" asked Jack. "What was he
wearing?"

"He was dressed in black," answered
Jean Paul. "His trousers were black, his
shirt was black, and his shoes were black.
I couldn't see his face, because his back
was towards me, but I could see that his
hair was the color of fire."

"He had red hair?" asked Jack, even
more curious. The description matched
the red hair Jack had found at the scene.

"Yes," said Jean Paul. "It was very bright
– just like those clowns in the circus.
Unmistakable," he muttered as his eyes
drifted off into the blue sky.

"Great," said Jack, "you've been really
helpful. I only need to do one more thing,

to rule you out as a suspect. Can I take a strand of your hair?"

Jean Paul looked at him, obviously confused. "I guess so," he said to Jack as he pulled one of his reddish-brown hairs from his head.

Jack reached back into his Book Bag and grabbed his DNA Decoder box. Opening it, he placed Jean Paul's hair next to the one he had found in the *Mona Lisa* room and

closed it. Punching the MATCH button on the box, he waited for it to tell him whether Jean Paul's hair and the one he found were from the same person.

When the words NO MATCH appeared, he turned to Jean Paul.

"Thanks for your help," he said. "You're no longer a suspect. I'll tell Chief Inspector Pierre that I have spoken to you. Would it be all right if we contacted you again?"

"Sure," said Jean Paul. "Can I go home now?"

"Sure can," said Jack, and he waved goodbye as the man walked off.

Jack thought about what Jean Paul had said. The person who stole the painting penetrated the security of the Louvre and did it without being noticed. Most importantly, this person had a glove with a built-in laser. Very few small-time crooks had access to that kind of technology.

Jack thought it was about time to pay a visit to the owner of the company responsible for security at the Louvre and understand more about what had happened last night. He rang Chief Inspector Pierre, who told him the man in question was Denis Dupré, owner of Paris Sécurité on the Champs Elysées.

Jack consulted his map and set off with questions still buzzing in his head. He hoped that after talking to Denis Dupré things would be clearer and he'd be closer to solving the mystery of the *Mona Lisa*.

Chapter 8:
The Big Cheese

The Champs Elysées is a famous street in Paris that leads down to another notable landmark, the Arc de Triomphe. Jack had seen the massive concrete arch of the Arc de Triomphe as he was running after Jean Paul. He walked up to the Paris Sécurité building and into the grand reception area.

Seated at the reception desk was a young woman with short, spiky black hair and a diamond nose ring. She was chewing gum so loudly that Jack could hear the pop and snap of every chew from the moment he entered the building.

"Hi there," Jack said to her. "I am here to see Denis Dupré."

She stared at Jack for a moment and then began to blow the biggest bubble that he had ever seen. It grew until it covered her entire face, then burst with a pop into the air.

"Do you have an appointment?" she said, using her tongue to gather the deflated gum back into her mouth.

Jack wondered if she were usually this professional. "No, but I am investigating the disappearance of the *Mona Lisa* for Chief Inspector Pierre," said Jack. "I am hoping he will agree to see me."

She picked up a phone and dialed a number. "Someone is here to see you about the *Mona Lisa*," she said into the receiver. There was a pause. She glanced up at Jack.

"He'll see you," she said, chewing and popping her gum again. "Take the elevator to the third floor. His office is down the hall."

Jack did as she instructed, got out of the elevator, and hurried down the hallway towards Monsieur Dupré's office. It wasn't hard to find, as the office took up half of the entire floor. Jack knocked.

"What do you want?" boomed a voice from the other side.

Jack opened the large double doors and found Monsieur Dupré finishing off his lunch – an entire spit-roasted chicken on a plate. Monsieur Dupré was a burly man, almost the size of the desk he was sitting behind. His fingers were greasy from handling the chicken, and bits of his meal were smeared across his face.

"Hello there," said Jack, careful not to extend his hand and get it covered with grease. "I am investigating the disappearance of the *Mona Lisa*. Since your firm handles the security for the Louvre, I thought I should speak to you."

"About what?!" Monsieur Dupré bellowed.

"Well, I would like to know more about your firm and who was working on the night of the theft," Jack explained.

"The police have already spoken to us," Monsieur Dupré said, snapping off a chicken wing and sending parts of his lunch splattering across the room. "Why should I speak to *you*?"

"I am running a separate investigation on behalf of the police and would appreciate any information you could provide," Jack answered politely. "Chief Inspector Pierre told me you'd be helpful." He forced a smile.

Monsieur Dupré groaned, annoyed that Jack had interrupted his lunch. "Look, kid, we're the largest security firm in Paris. We specialize in security for some of the top museums in the city. We handle the Louvre, the Musée d'Orsay and, of course, the Pompidou. All of our security officers are well-trained and reliable. It's a pity that the *Mona Lisa* was stolen, but I can assure you we had nothing to do with it."

"Maybe you didn't, sir," said Jack, "but perhaps someone who works for you knows something."

"That's rubbish! I am Denis Dupré, owner of this firm," he roared, raising his voice and slamming his grimy fists down on the desk, "and I don't hire any crooks!"

Jack could tell that Monsieur Dupré was a bit sensitive – after all, by now most of the world was blaming his firm for not taking better care of the *Mona Lisa*. But Jack needed to speak to Monsieur Dupré's security officers to find out if they knew or had seen anything. He wasn't about to give up now just because the boss was having a tantrum.

"I'm not suggesting that your firm doesn't have a good reputation," Jack said soothingly. "It's just that it might be helpful to speak to the officer who was on duty last night."

"He's unavailable," bristled Monsieur Dupré. "He was questioned so much last night that I gave him the day off."

"Well unfortunately I still need to speak to him today," said Jack. "Can you ask him to call me as soon as he can? He can reach me through Chief Inspector Pierre's office. I'm sure you understand how important it is to solve this crime as quickly as possible."

"Yes. Well, OK," said Monsieur Dupré, settling down.

"Thanks for your time," said Jack as he walked towards the double doors. Just as he was leaving the room, something caught his eye. A row of photographs hung on the wall and in one of them there was a man with bright red hair.

That's an odd coincidence, thought Jack. Thoughts started to pop into his head. "Excuse me," he said to Monsieur Dupré, pointing to the red-haired man, "what is his name?"

"That's Carl Ponte," said Monsieur Dupré, clearing his throat.

"Was he working at the Louvre last night?" Jack asked.

"As a matter of fact," said Monsieur

Dupré, "he was. He was guarding the
Ancient Egypt room. Carl's an excellent
security guard," he added. "He's newly
qualified and a specialist in surveillance.
He's over at the Musée d'Orsay right now.
They've asked him to take a look at their
systems in light of what happened last
night."

"That's probably a good idea," agreed
Jack, starting to think that Carl's working
at the Louvre last night might have been

more than a coincidence. "Thanks for your help." He opened the doors to Monsieur Dupré's office and hurried out. *"Au revoir!"*

As Jack walked down the hall and towards the elevator, he thought about what he'd learned from Denis Dupré. If Jack's hunch were right, then this security guard named Carl probably had something to do with the theft of the painting. But there was no way Jack could arrest him without solid evidence. He needed to speak to Carl first and figure out whether his theory was right.

Jack opened his map and found the location of the Musée d'Orsay. There was no time to walk. He needed a cab. He dashed through the entrance of the building and out onto the street. He lifted his arm and hailed the first taxi in sight.

"I need to get to the Musée d'Orsay –

and fast!" said Jack to the taxi driver as
he climbed into the car.

"*Oui!*" said the man as he slammed his
foot on the accelerator and sped down
the Champs Elysées.

Chapter 9:
The Red-Haired Man

Within minutes, the taxi arrived at the
front of the Musée d'Orsay, a converted
train station located close to the River
Seine. Jack jumped out and rushed inside.
There was a group of security officers
chatting in the reception area. One of
them turned towards him.

"The museum's closed today, young
man," he said.

"I know," said Jack, flashing his GPF
badge. "I am here to see one of the
security officers on duty. Can you tell me
where I can find Carl Ponte?" he asked.

"Sure thing," another officer said. "He's in the Monet room testing the surveillance equipment. Quite a famous painter, that Monet," the man rambled on. "We have lots of his paintings in that room. They are worth quite a bit of money, which is why Carl—"

"Nice to know," said Jack, interrupting the man. "Where exactly is the Monet room?" he asked.

"Top floor," explained the guard. "There's an elevator at the back of the museum."

Jack said a quick thank-you and hurried down the hall. He took the elevator to the top floor and followed the signs to the Monet room. He rounded the corner and began to enter, but stopped short at the door. Something was moving inside.

Jack peeked around the corner. A tall man, dressed in black with flaming red hair, was standing before one of the paintings. It was a lovely picture of a field filled with red flowers. As Jack watched, he placed his hands on either side of the painting and gently lifted it off the wall, then placed it on the ground. The man looked over his shoulder to see whether anyone was coming, but didn't spot Jack. He gently wrapped the painting in brown paper.

Next, the red-haired man took a small box out of his pocket and threw it on the floor. Instantly the box grew to three times its size, large enough for the painting to fit inside. He placed the painting in the box and put a sticker on it that said: HI-TECH SECURITY EQUIPMENT. Then he climbed the ladder near the security camera and reconnected some wires.

Once he was back on the floor he reached for a walkie-talkie that was clipped to his belt.

"Philippe, it's Carl. I've finished rewiring the camera in the Monet room so it shouldn't be flickering now."

He's planning to sneak the painting out of here under everyone's nose! Jack thought to himself.

"Stop!" commanded Jack, entering the room and flashing his badge. "By order of the Global Protection Force, I demand that you surrender yourself and return that painting to its rightful place."

"Yeah, right, kid," the man sneered at Jack as he picked up the box and ran out of the room.

"Thief!" yelled Jack, dashing off to follow the man. "Someone is trying to steal one of the Monet paintings!"

The red-haired man raced along the

corridor and down a flight of stairs. Jack
was trying his hardest to catch him. But
the man was so fast, he was getting away.

"He's heading towards the entrance!"
shouted Jack as he bolted down the stairs
and onto the ground floor. "Stop him!" he

yelled to the guards. But they were too involved in their own conversation to register what Jack was saying. The red-haired man raced past the guards, knocking one of the men off his feet and onto the ground.

"Somebody, stop him!" yelled Jack again as he sprinted out of the door. By then the guards had understood what Jack was saying and rushed to join him.

Carl Ponte darted through the crowds outside the museum and ran into the road. Waiting for him was a white van with the words CHANNEL FERRIES written on it. The passenger door flew open and the red-haired man jumped inside. The driver slammed his foot on the accelerator and the van screeched off just as Jack reached the curb.

Panting breathlessly, Jack looked at the van and its registration plate. The

first two numbers and letter were 82 W. Because the van was moving so fast, Jack couldn't see anything else.

"Channel Ferries, huh?" said one of the officers as he caught up with Jack. "I've done work with them before. They're a ferry service between Calais here in France and Dover in England. The ferry

crosses the Channel twice a day. The next crossing," he added, looking at his watch, "leaves in four hours."

"That must be what he is doing," Jack thought aloud. "Transporting the paintings out of the country in order to sell them. I need to be on that ferry."

Jack tapped a few numbers on his Watch Phone. "Chief Inspector Pierre," he said, speaking into his wrist, "we've had another theft. Pick me up at the Musée d'Orsay. We're going to Calais."

Chapter 10:
The Hull

Henri came to collect Jack in an unmarked car and they sped the whole way from the museum in Paris to the port in Calais. When they arrived, they positioned themselves at the departure point, where cars and trucks drove onto the ramp and into the boat.

The ferry itself was divided into two main sections – the hull, which held the cars and trucks below, and the passenger decks, which were on the upper levels. Once the ferry left the dock, no one was allowed to be in the hull or leave the upper decks to go down to their cars.

Over a hundred cars and trucks drove past Henri and Jack, but none looked like the van from the Musée d'Orsay. As Jack was thinking that perhaps Carl wasn't planning to take the paintings by boat, he spied a white van with a lone driver. He couldn't see the driver's face, but the van clearly said CHANNEL FERRIES and the registration number started with 82 W.

"Look! There it is!" said Jack, pointing to the van. "Let's get ourselves on this ferry."

Henri slowly drove up the ramp and into the ferry behind the van. The huge heavy door of the ferry closed with a boom behind them. Henri parked the car close to the vehicle and turned off the engine. Everything went quiet, except for the sound of the chief inspector quickly breathing in and out in anticipation of

what was going to happen next. Jack
could feel his heart pounding, too, as he
saw the door of the van open and a man
climb out.

Chapter 11:
The Desperate Struggle

"It's the red-haired man!" gasped the chief inspector as he watched the thief get out of the truck. The man locked the door and made his way to the stairs leading to the passenger decks.

"All passengers must be on the upper levels in thirty minutes," boomed a voice over the loudspeaker, "as the ferry will depart promptly at 17:00 hours."

"OK," said Jack, turning to Henri. "We have thirty minutes. Let's see what's in the van."

Jack and Henri got out of the car and carefully walked forwards. They tried to open the back doors of the truck, but as expected they were locked.

Jack rifled through his Secret Agent Book Bag and took out his Magic Key Maker. He inserted the long rubber stick into the keyhole. Instantly, the rubber hardened to form a key. Jack turned it and the lock popped open.

Henri and Jack pulled open the doors to reveal what was inside. Jack's eyes opened wide. Inside the van were lots of objects wrapped in brown paper, just like the paper he'd seen Carl use at the Musée d'Orsay. He picked up the nearest one and handed it to Henri.

The chief inspector opened the object with trembling hands. He gasped as he looked at a small statue of a ballerina. "It's a bronze statue by Rodin," he said. "It's been missing from the Rodin Museum for over two months!"

The next package was about the same size. The chief inspector unwrapped it and gasped again. "This one is an African mask from the Musée de l'Homme. We thought this had been broken into two pieces! This must be the original and the broken pieces are a hoax!"

Jack climbed further inside and spied what looked like a painting. He peeled back the wrapper to reveal a painting of a woman in a brown dress, folding her hands over her stomach and smiling at Jack.

"Oh my!" exclaimed Henri. "It's the *Mona Lisa*! Jack, we must be careful," he whispered cautiously. "The people who have stolen these pieces of artwork are very dangerous. They will probably do whatever it takes to prevent anyone from upsetting their plans."

Suddenly Chief Inspector Pierre

snapped his head around in the direction of the stairs leading to the upper levels. He turned back to Jack. He looked frightened. "He's back! Quickly, Jack, you must get out of the—"

THWACK! Something came down heavily on the chief inspector's head and he collapsed onto the floor outside the van. The red-haired man stepped from behind Henri with a club in his right hand.

"We meet again, kid," he sneered. "But this time you're really going to regret coming after me."

Jack froze. The man gave an evil laugh and went to slam the doors closed.

"No!" cried Jack, diving towards him. But it was too late. He crashed into the doors, knocking his Watch Phone against them as they shut, trapping him inside.

Chapter 12:
The Darkness

Jack squinted his eyes and tried to see through the darkness. Thankfully, there was a little light coming from an air vent above. He looked at his Watch Phone, but it wasn't working. He must have banged it a bit too hard, he reckoned, when he crashed into the doors trying to get Carl.

Jack paused for a minute and tried to think of what to do. He thought of Max and what his brother would do in a situation like this. Since Max was taller than Jack, he figured he'd probably try to get out through the vent above.

"That's it!" Jack said to himself. Although he couldn't reach the vent from where he was, he knew he had a gadget that could help him do it. He reached into his bag and fumbled around. He took out what felt like an ordinary piece of wood, but Jack knew this was the GPF's Ratchet Step. He placed it on the floor and stood on top.

"Six steps, please," Jack commanded. *CLICK. CLICK. CLICK.* The piece of wood built itself upwards into the form of a ladder. It was just high enough to lift Jack up to the hole.

Unfortunately he was too big to fit through, but Jack had another idea. He ejected his Melting Ink Pen from the side of his Watch Phone and placed it on the ceiling of the van. He drew a circle around the vent. The ink from the pen melted through the steel and Jack quietly pulled himself out of the van and onto the roof.

He looked out across the hull and towards the back of the van. He could see Chief Inspector Pierre unconscious on the floor with the club lying beside him, but there was no sign of the red-haired man. Although his watch didn't work, Jack figured he had about fifteen minutes before the ferry departed. Frustratingly, he wasn't even close to capturing Carl.

Jack carefully climbed down the back of the truck and knelt down beside Henri. He reached into his pocket and pulled out a small tub of Time-Release Vapors, then rubbed some under Henri's nose.

"That should help you to wake up shortly," whispered Jack. Just then, he heard the red-haired man's voice coming from the front of the van.

"Yeah, the kid is here," Carl said. "I've got him in the back of the van. Not sure what I am going to do with him and the inspector. I don't really want anyone else from the GPF on our tail. Any suggestions, boss?"

Boss, thought Jack. So there is someone else behind this.

"Right, no problem," continued Carl. "I'll get rid of them. I'll toss them into the sea during the voyage. Speak to you when I reach Dover."

Jack heard the click as Carl hung up.
Then he seemed to be fumbling for
something in the front seat of the van.
Jack had to act quickly, or he and Henri
were toast.

Jack climbed back onto the top of the
van. He saw Carl open the front door
and step out with a rope in his hands.
The thief made his way towards the back
of the truck and the chief inspector.

Carl knelt down beside Henri,
who was still unconscious,
and snapped the rope
tight between his two
hands. Just as Carl
was about to wrap
the rope around his
neck, Henri's eyes
opened. The Time-
Release Vapors had
worked!

"Get off me, you thief!" Henri shouted at the red-haired man. The chief inspector grabbed the rope and struggled with the man for control. With one swift move, Carl grabbed his club and whacked Henri on the head again, knocking him unconscious for a second time.

Chapter 13:
The Deadly Glove

"Leave him alone!" screamed Jack from above as he jumped onto the man's back.

Carl Ponte stood up quickly, throwing Jack off his back and onto the floor. "That will teach you, you little brat!" He scowled.

From the back pocket of his trousers, Carl pulled out a black glove and put it on his right hand. Out of his fingertips shot five red lasers. He aimed the glove in Jack's direction.

Quickly, Jack dived between two cars.

ZAP! The lasers sliced through the front
end of one of the cars.

"Come here, kid. Let me show you how
this laser really works," Carl sniggered.
Jack scurried between the cars.

"You can't get away from me, you little

punk," he said, now running in Jack's direction.

Jack could hear the whirr of the laser coming closer. He hurried down the line of vehicles and hid behind a red truck.

"You can't hide for ever," the man growled.

Jack rummaged desperately through his Book Bag. "Where is it? Where is it!?" he muttered to himself. He was searching for the one thing that might be able to save him. "That's it!" he said aloud as he pulled the life-saving gadget out of his bag. He took a deep breath and stood up from behind the red truck. He looked directly at the red-haired man.

"OK, Carl!" Jack yelled. "Give me all you've got!"

Chapter 14:
The Hypno-Disc

The red-haired man lifted his glove and aimed the razor-sharp lasers at Jack. Instantly, Jack raised his left hand. In it was a round, flat disk with swirls of color.

Jack was holding the mother of all secret-agent gadgets: the Hypno-Disk. Normally, the Hypno-Disk would spin in a clockwise direction, throwing out a light that, when seen, would hypnotize someone on the spot. But Jack had activated the reverse mechanism. Instead of sending out light, the Hypno-Disk was sucking in all the light from Carl's deadly laser glove, making it useless.

Carl stood facing Jack with a look of panic on his face. The red-haired man had failed in his attempt to kill Jack, and now Jack had all the power.

The evil villain looked closely at the Hypno-Disk. He had never seen one before, but he had heard about its powers. The red-haired man gulped and did what any sensible criminal would do: he dropped to the floor and began pleading for mercy.

"Please don't hurt me, kid," Carl begged. "I didn't mean it. I was just doing what I was told to do."

Jack thought for a moment. He would never kill Carl, but it didn't hurt to make him squirm. "I suppose I could spare your life," he said, "if you tell me who you are working for and why you've been stealing these important pieces of art."

Just then, Jack heard a noise from
behind Carl's van.

"Oh, my head!" groaned the voice.
"What happened?" It was Chief Inspector
Pierre. He pulled himself up and looked
around. "Are you OK, Jack?" he called
over.

"Sure am, Chief Inspector," replied Jack.

Henri ambled over to join Jack, rubbing
the bump on his head.

"It was my boss, Denis Dupré, who made me do this," confessed Carl, sobbing into his hands. "He told me that if I helped him steal these precious pieces of art, he would give me one million euros so that I could repay my debts. He was planning to sell them to private collectors living in other countries—"

"But surely," interrupted Chief Inspector

Pierre, "someone would have seen these works and arrested the people who bought them."

"These works of art were for very special private collections," explained Carl, "so no one but the owners would have seen them."

"How were you able to steal the *Mona Lisa* without anyone knowing?" asked Jack.

"Monsieur Dupré had it arranged that the guard on duty would turn off the surveillance equipment between 7:50 and 7:55 p.m.," explained Carl. "That way, I could steal the painting and there would be no record of my entering or exiting the room." Carl looked pleadingly at Henri and Jack.

"Well," said Jack to Henri, "what should we do with him?"

Chief Inspector Pierre walked behind Carl. He grabbed Carl's wrists and held

them behind his back. Out of his pocket
he pulled a pair of handcuffs. He dragged
Carl into a standing position and clamped
them onto his wrists.

"For now," said the chief inspector,
looking at his watch, "I think we should
get off this boat and hand him to the port
authorities. We have bigger fish to fry," he
added. "Denis Dupré is responsible for
this. I think it's time we paid him a visit
together."

Chapter 15:
The Big Cheese
Revisited

Jack and the chief inspector walked into the glass atrium of the Paris Sécurité office on the Champs Elysées. They marched past the woman at the front desk, who was busily reading a book and chewing away at her gum. By the time she had noticed them they had already entered the elevator and were on their way up to the third floor.

Jack and Henri walked down the hallway towards Monsieur Dupré's office. Without knocking, Chief Inspector Pierre flung open the door. Monsieur Dupré was sitting at his desk with his back facing Jack and Henri. He was so engrossed in a phone conversation that he didn't even hear them enter the room.

"Yes, that's right," said Monsieur Dupré into the receiver. "You can have the actual *Mona Lisa* by that artist Da . . . Da . . . Da . . . Yeah, that's the one . . . for the reasonable price of one hundred million euros."

"Ahem!" coughed Henri, in an attempt to get Monsieur Dupré's attention.

"Huh?" said Monsiuer Dupré as he looked over his shoulder. When he saw that it was Jack and the chief inspector, he spun his chair around so fast that he banged his knee on the corner of the desk. "Owwww!" he howled in pain. Hunched over the desk and rubbing his knee, he slowly put the receiver down.

"I arrest you, Denis Dupré, for masterminding the theft of the *Mona Lisa* and the other works of art found in Carl Ponte's possession," declared Chief Inspector Pierre as he walked behind the desk to handcuff Denis.

"What? This is ridiculous!" shouted Monsieur Dupré, standing up in protest. "I am Denis Dupré, owner of this firm, and I had nothing to do with anything! That phone call," he said, trying to explain

what Jack and Henri had overheard, "I . . .
I . . . I . . . was just pretending. I don't
know anything about the *Mona Lisa*!"

"That's not what your accomplice, Carl
Ponte, said," remarked Henri as he placed
the handcuffs on the man's wrists. "He
has identified you as the mastermind
behind the operation. And I believe him."
Chief Inspector Pierre pulled Monsieur
Dupré from behind his desk and over to
Jack.

"This is because of you, isn't it?" growled Denis angrily at Jack.

"Yep," said Jack, "and I hope that you have learned your lesson. You should never take something that doesn't belong to you."

"You little—" The big man turned red with rage as he lunged towards him.

"Thanks, Jack," said Henri, holding out his hand to shake Jack's. "We couldn't have done this without you. The city of Paris is especially grateful."

"No problem," said Jack. "I'm glad that I was able to help. You know where to find me if you need me again," he offered.

"Let's hope we don't," replied Henri, "but you know you're welcome in France anytime."

Jack smiled at him and tried to avoid the evil glares from Monsieur Dupré.

"Now, let's see if we can find a comfortable cell for you to spend a nice long holiday in," the chief inspector said to Denis as he led him down the hall.

Henri waved to Jack as he and Monsieur Dupré stepped into the elevator. Jack waved back.

Chapter 16:
The Lift Home

Well, I guess it's time for me to get home, Jack thought to himself.

He walked over to the second elevator and pushed the down button. The doors sprang open and Jack stepped inside. Out of his Book Bag he pulled a round button with the letter H on it and placed it over the G for ground floor. He pushed it and the button began to glow.

"Home, please," said Jack to the button, and the elevator began to move downwards. As it descended, he yelled, "Off to England!"

When the doors opened again, Jack found himself in the middle of his bedroom, just as he had left it. As he stepped out of the elevator it vanished behind him. He walked over to his clock and looked at the time: 7:31 PM. Perfect, he thought as he walked over to his desk. He picked up the unfinished drawing of his comic-book hero, Super Smash, and sat down.

"Now," said Jack, "it's time to finish him off."

Jack lifted his pencil and began to draw. He knew his sketch would never be as famous as some of the works of art he saw in Paris. But he didn't care. Art, after all, Jack reckoned, wasn't about fame, it was about fun. And that's just what Jack was doing now—having a blast drawing Super Smash destroying Tortua with a powerful disk that stole her power. Now that, thought Jack, is a great idea.

The Caper of the
Crown Jewels:
ENGLAND
BOOK ④

The Caper
of the
Crown Jewels:
ENGLAND

Elizabeth Singer Hunt

Illustrated by Brian Williamson

WEINSTEIN
BOOKS

ISBN: 1-60286-013-0
ISBN 13: 978-1-60286-013-1

First Edition
10   9   8   7   6   5

*For the children who supported
Jack and me in the early days*

THE WORLD

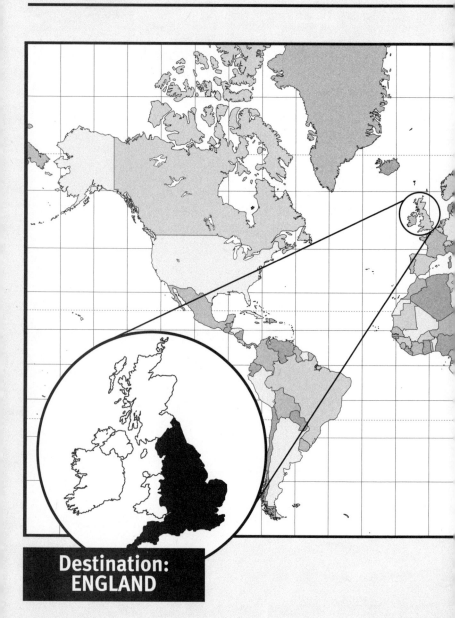

**Destination:
ENGLAND**

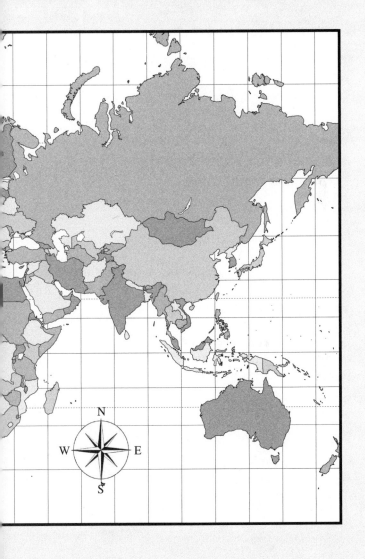

JACK STALWART

Jack Stalwart applied to be a secret agent for the Global Protection Force four months ago.

My name is Jack Stalwart. My older brother, Max, was a secret agent for you, until he disappeared on one of your missions. Now I want to be a secret agent, too. If you choose me, I will be an excellent secret agent and get rid of evil villains, just like my brother did.

Sincerely,

Jack Stalwart

HIGHLY CONFIDENTIAL

Jack Stalwart was sworn in as a Global Protection Force secret agent four months ago. Since that time, he has completed all of his missions successfully and has stopped no less than twelve evil villains. Because of this he has been assigned the code name COURAGE.

Jack has yet to uncover the whereabouts of his brother, Max, who is still working for this organization at a secret location. Do not give Secret Agent Jack Stalwart this information. He is never to know about his brother.

Gerald Barter

Gerald Barter
Director, Global Protection Force

THINGS YOU'LL FIND IN EVERY BOOK

Watch Phone: The only gadget Jack wears all the time, even when he's not on official business. His Watch Phone is the central gadget that makes most others work. There are lots of important features, most importantly the C button, which reveals the code of the day—necessary to unlock Jack's Secret Agent Book Bag. There are buttons on both sides, one of which ejects his life-saving Melting Ink Pen. Beyond these functions, it also works as a phone and, of course, gives Jack the time of day.

Global Protection Force (GPF): The GPF is the organization Jack works for. It's a worldwide force of young secret agents whose aim is to protect the world's people, places, and possessions. No one knows exactly where its main offices are located (all correspondence and gadgets for repair are sent to a special PO Box, and training is held at various locations around the world), but Jack thinks it's somewhere cold, like the Arctic Circle.

Whizzy: Jack's magical miniature globe. Almost every night at precisely 7:30 PM, the GPF uses Whizzy to send Jack the identity of the country that he must travel to. Whizzy can't talk, but he can cough up messages. Jack's parents don't know Whizzy is anything more than a normal globe.

The Magic Map: The magical map hanging on Jack's bedroom wall. Unlike most maps, the GPF's map is made of a mysterious wood. Once Jack inserts the country piece from Whizzy, the map swallows Jack whole and sends him away on his missions. When he returns, he arrives precisely one minute after he left.

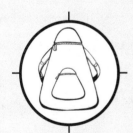

Secret Agent Book Bag: The Book Bag that Jack wears on every adventure. Licensed only to GPF secret agents, it contains top-secret gadgets necessary to foil bad guys and escape certain death. To activate the bag before each mission, Jack must punch in a secret code given to him by his Watch Phone. Once he's away, all he has to do is place his finger on the zipper, which identifies him as the owner of the bag and it immediately opens.

THE STALWART FAMILY

Jack's dad, John

He moved the family to England when Jack was two, in order to take a job with an aerospace company. As far as Jack knows, his dad designs and manufactures airplane parts. Jack's dad thinks he is an ordinary boy and that his other son, Max, attends a school in Switzerland. Jack's dad is American and his mum is British, which makes Jack a bit of both.

Jack's mum, Corinne

One of the greatest mums as far as Jack is concerned. When she and her husband received a letter from a posh school in Switzerland inviting Max to attend, they were overjoyed. Since Max left six months ago, they have received numerous notes in Max's handwriting telling them he's OK. Little do they know it's all a lie and that it's the GPF sending those letters.

Jack's older brother, Max

Two years ago, at the age of nine, Max joined the GPF. Max used to tell Jack about his adventures and show him how to work his secret-agent gadgets. When the family received a letter inviting Max to attend a school in Europe, Jack figured it was to do with the GPF. Max told him he was right, but that he couldn't tell Jack anything about why he was going away.

Nine-year-old Jack Stalwart

Four months ago, Jack received an anonymous note saying: "Your brother is in danger. Only you can save him." As soon as he could, Jack applied to be a secret agent, too. Since that time, he's battled some of the world's most dangerous villains and hopes some day in his travels to find and rescue his brother, Max.

DESTINATION:
England

Great Britain is made up of three countries: England, Scotland and Wales.

□

Its capital city, London, is one of the most famous cities in the world.

□

Big Ben, Westminster Abbey, the Houses of Parliament, the London Eye, Buckingham Palace, and the Tower of London are located there.

□

The two "houses" of Parliament, the House of Commons and the House of Lords, have been around since the Middle Ages.

The London "Eye" is actually an enormous Ferris wheel located next to the River Thames.

□

Queen Elizabeth II is one of the longest reigning monarchs in British history. She has ruled for over fifty years.

□

The Queen's jewels—the Crown Jewels—are housed in the Tower of London.

The Great Travel Guide

THE TOWER OF LONDON: A HISTORY

The Tower of London has been the home and fortress of the British monarchy for nearly 900 years.

It's not one tower, but a series of towers, buildings, walled walks and lawns.

Throughout history, the Tower has been used as a treasury, zoo, prison, and weapons storehouse.

Prisoners arrived at the Tower by boating down the River Thames and passing underneath Traitors' Gate.

Today, the Tower serves as a tourist attraction where people can learn about its history and see the Queen's Crown Jewels.

THE CROWN JEWELS:
Facts and Figures

The Crown Jewels is the name given to the ceremonial crowns, orbs, scepters (pronounced *sep-ters*), plates, spoons, rings, and clothing used by the British monarchy.

◆

Many of the pieces were made in the 1600s during the reign of Charles II.

◆

Except for three swords and a spoon, all regalia made before the reign of Charles II was destroyed in 1649 at Oliver Cromwell's command.

The largest cut diamond in the world, the Cullinan I, sits on top of the Sovereign's Scepter with Cross. It weighs 530 carats.

◆

Queen Elizabeth II wears the Imperial State Crown at the opening of Parliament. It was made in 1937.

◆

Since the fourteenth century, the Crown Jewels have been kept at the Tower of London. During the Second World War, they were moved to a secret hiding place.

THE YEOMAN WARDER

Yeoman Warders are also known as Beefeaters.

Their legendary life at the Tower began more than 500 years ago. They were responsible for guarding the Tower of London and its prisoners.

Today, their role is similar, although they don't watch over prisoners anymore. Instead, they give guided tours on the Tower's history.

One of the Yeoman Warders, the Ravenmaster, takes care of the Tower's blackbirds. Legend has it that if the ravens leave, the monarchy will fall.

MAGIC FINGERS

You will need:
A cup of water
Black pepper
A bar of soap

Before the trick:
Rub the bar of soap
over one of your fingers.

The trick:
Take the cup of water and sprinkle lots
of black pepper on the top. Ask for a
volunteer to dip a finger in and try to
push the pepper away; it will only stick
to the fingers.

Then tell everyone you've got magic
fingers. Lean over the cup, wiggle your
fingers and say "Presto Pepper!" Slowly
lower the finger with soap on it into
the water and watch as the pepper
magically separates!

★ ☆ ★ ☆ ★ ☆ ★ ☆

DISAPPEARING COIN

You will need:
2 sheets of colored paper
A clear glass
A coin
A handkerchief
A wand or pencil
Clear sticky tape

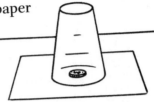

Before the trick:
Turn the glass upside down onto the first piece of colored paper. Trace the rim and cut the circle out. Then tape it to the mouth of the glass, trying to make the tape invisible.

The trick:
Put the other sheet of paper on a table with the coin and upside-down glass next to each other. Tell everyone that you're going to make the coin disappear. Place the handkerchief over the glass. Carefully lift and slide the glass on top of the coin and tap it with the wand. Say "Abracadabra!" and lift the handkerchief. The coin's disappeared!

SECRET AGENT GADGET INSTRUCTION MANUAL

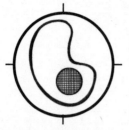

Ear Amp: When you need to listen in on some crooks or figure out if there's trouble ahead, use the Ear Amp. The GPF's Ear Amp looks like a kidney bean but is one of the most sophisticated hearing devices in the world. Just hook it onto your ear and you can hear conversations from afar or through walls. No battery required.

Tornado: Acting like a catapult, the GPF's Tornado is the ideal gadget for catching up to three villains on the run. Just select the number of ropes required and pull the trigger. With the force of a tornado, the ropes will be flung out, wrapping up your enemies within seconds.

Rock Corer:

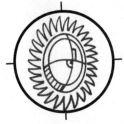

For any secret agent working underground, the Rock Corer is essential. Just pick up this circular saw and twist it, so that its teeth open to the size that you want. Carefully place it against the rock and pull the small lever on its side. Within minutes, it will have created a tunnel for crawling through or a hole for getting much-needed air.

Encryption Notebook:

When you need to keep your notes top-secret, use the GPF's Encryption Notebook (EN). It looks like an ordinary handheld device, but it can change what you write into complete gibberish. Touch the panel marked ENCRYPT.

NOTE: Thumbprint identification is necessary for EN activation. Please make sure yours has been registered at GPF HQ before using for the first time.

Chapter 1:
The Magic Break

It was a rainy day on the 9th of May and Jack Stalwart was sitting at his desk in his bedroom doing his homework. His fourth-grade class was studying the history of the British Empire. In front of him was a long list of British kings and queens who had ruled the country since the time of William the Conqueror. He looked at the list and his eyes glazed over.

"There's no way I'm going to memorize these names by tomorrow." He sighed.

Kings and Queens of Great Britain

(since William the Conqueror)

Normans	Dates
William I (the Conqueror)	1066–1087
William II (Rufus)	1087–1100
Henry I	1100–1135
Stephen	1135–1154
Plantagenets	
Henry II	1154–1189
Richard I (Lionheart)	1189–1199
John (Lackland)	1199–1216
Henry III	1216–1272
Edward I (Longshanks)	1272–1307
Edward II	1307–1327
Edward III	1327–1377
Richard II	1377–1399
Lancaster	
Henry IV	1399–1413
Henry V	1413–1422
Henry VI	1422–1461
York	
Edward IV	1461–1483
Edward V	1483
Richard III	1483–1485
Tudor	
Henry VII	1485–1509
Henry VIII	1509–1547
Edward VI	1547–1553
Mary I	1553–1558
Elizabeth I	1558–1603
Stuart	
James I	1603–1625
Charles I	1625–1649
The Commonwealth	1649–1660
Charles II	1660–1685
James II	1685–1688
William III and Mary II	1689–1702
Anne	1702–1714
Hanover	
George I	1714–1727
George II	1727–1760
George III	1760–1820
George IV	1820–1830
William IV	1830–1837
Victoria	1837–1901
Saxe-Coburg-Gotha	
Edward VII	1901–1910
Windsor	
George V	1910–1936
Edward VIII	1936
George VI	1936–1952
Elizabeth II	1952–

"There are too many of them." Jack closed the book and decided to take a break.

He walked over to his bedside table and opened the top drawer. Inside was one of his favorite books: *Master the Art of Magic.* He pulled it out, sat on his bed, and began to read the section called "Appearing Coin" on page thirty-one. Jack smiled to himself. This was much more fun than homework.

Ever since Jack's Uncle Richard had taken him to see the master magician, Ivan the Incredible, in London, he'd been fascinated by the art of illusion. He'd watched as the magician made an enormous elephant disappear right on stage. Towards the end of the show, he'd escaped from a straitjacket while hanging over a fiery pit. "Incredible" was the right word. Jack had never seen anything like it before.

As soon as he got home that night, Jack had asked his mum for a book on magic. On his birthday, she surprised him with *Master the Art of Magic*. It was the biggest selling book on magic and, in Jack's opinion, just about the best. Every page was chock-full of exciting tips on how to fool your friends and family with magical tricks. Last night, he had learned how to bend a spoon. Tonight, he was going to learn how to pull a coin out of thin air.

Jack reached into his top drawer and grabbed some sticky tape. Then he pulled a coin out of his trouser pocket. Cutting off a piece of tape, he stuck the coin onto the back of his first finger. Doing as the book said, he reached behind his ear and then flipped his middle finger forward. The coin magically appeared in the palm of his hand.

"Fantastic!" shouted Jack. "My friends at school are going to love this one!" At that, there was a knock on the door.

"How's the homework going?" said a familiar voice from the other side. It was Jack's mum checking up on his progress.

"Uh, all right, Mum," said Jack, putting the coin in his pocket and racing back to his desk.

"That's great, honey," his mum said through the door. "Don't forget to brush your teeth before you go to bed."

"OK, Mum," said Jack. He hoped his mum wouldn't ask to come in.

She didn't, and when he was sure that she'd made her way back downstairs, Jack pulled the coin out of his trouser pocket. "Now," he said, "let's practice that trick again."

Chapter 2:
The Land of Kings
and Queens

At that moment, Jack's miniature globe began to spin on top of his bedside table. Hearing this, Jack put his magic book away. There were more important things to concentrate on now. It was 7:30 PM.

Jack was a Secret Agent for the Global Protection Force. The Global Protection Force, or GPF, was a worldwide group of young secret agents determined to fight crime and protect the world's most precious treasures. When Jack was sworn in by the GPF a couple of years ago, he chose as his globe a little one called Whizzy. Although Whizzy couldn't talk, he could give Jack clues about his next mission by spitting jigsaw pieces from his mouth. Since it was precisely 7:30 PM, that's exactly what Whizzy was going to do.

Whizzy coughed: "Ahem!" A small jigsaw piece flew out of his mouth and across the room. It bounced off the wall and landed on the floor. Jack bent over and looked to see whether he recognized the shape of the country.

"No way," said Jack. "I can't believe it!" he added, looking at its unmistakable form. "That's where I live."

Jack raced to the Magic Map on his bedroom wall. It was a brilliant map of the world, with every country in bright colors. Jack placed the jigsaw piece exactly where he knew it belonged and watched as the name "England" appeared on the map.

From inside the country, a red light began to glow. Jack pulled his Book Bag out from under his bed and checked his Watch Phone for the code of the day. After receiving it, he punched the word— Q-U-E-E-N—into the bag's lock. Almost instantly, it opened, revealing what was tucked inside.

In addition to the usual gadgets, there was the Encryption Notebook, the Ear Amp, and the Tornado. The GPF had just added the Heli-Spacer, a device that enabled you to fly using your hands to control your direction. Although Jack hadn't needed it yet, he was hoping he'd get a chance to use it on this mission.

Jack closed his Book Bag and ran over to the map. As the light from inside the country grew to fill his room, he smiled and yelled, "Off to England!"

With those words, the red light burst,
swallowing him into the Magic Map.

Chapter 3:
The Tower of Infamy

As soon as Jack arrived, he was aware of something sinister above him. He quickly hit the ground, rolled over twice, and got himself out of harm's way. Looking up, Jack noticed a row of iron spikes hanging inside a rounded arch.

"Don't worry," said a male voice from behind him. "The only way that portcullis comes down is if I let it down." Jack knew that the word *portcullis* meant a gate or grating that slid up and down.

Jack whipped round. Standing nearby

was a man
dressed in a
long blue
jacket with a
red crown and
two letters—
E and *R*—
embroidered on its
chest. He also had a
red and gold badge
attached to his
arm. Because of
the way he was
dressed, Jack knew
not only what the
man was but also
where he was. The
man was a Yeoman
Warder, a legendary
protector of the
Tower of London.

"You must be Jack," he said. "The GPF said they'd be sending you. My name is Tommy," he added. "I'm one of the Yeoman Warders."

Jack took a good look at Tommy—the GPF trained him to look at details. He was middle-aged, of average build, and had grey hairs sprouting within his brown beard.

"Nice to meet you," said Jack, excited to be speaking to a real Yeoman Warder. He was fascinated by the history of the Tower of London and had been there several times with his mum and dad. He knew that Yeoman Warders were sometimes called *Beefeaters* because in the old days they were probably paid their wages in beef.

Jack looked past Tommy to the cobblestone street ahead. Because he'd been here before, he knew that the Tower of London was a popular tourist attraction. Hundreds of tourists usually filled the streets. Today, however, there was no one around.

"What's wrong?" asked Jack, figuring something bad must have happened if there weren't any visitors.

"Well," said Tommy, taking off his hat and scratching his bald head. "We have a slight problem." Before Jack could respond, he added, "Someone has stolen the Crown Jewels. And between you and me"—he leaned towards Jack—"the Queen's not pleased."

Chapter 4:
The Caper

"What?" said Jack, who was completely shocked. "I can't believe someone's stolen the Crown Jewels!"

"Neither can I," said Tommy, his face looking serious.

"Have you contacted Scotland Yard or MI5?" asked Jack, referring to the country's finest law-enforcement agencies.

"Not yet," he said. "The Queen's given the Warders four hours to locate the crooks before she notifies them herself."

"How could this have happened?" asked Jack.

"I don't know," said Tommy. "It's very embarrassing. The Jewel House is locked up tighter than you would believe. We have some pretty hi-tech security equipment in there," he added. "The jewels were there one second and gone the next. We've even looked at the footage from the security cameras."

"What did you see?" said Jack, anxious to know whether there were any clues on the tapes.

"There were six people viewing the jewels at that time," explained Tommy. "Out of nowhere, the lights went out, which meant our cameras couldn't pick up a thing. When they came back on, the same six people were there, looking

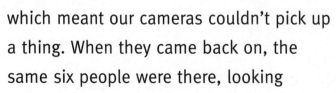

17

stunned. We've searched them," he went on, "and none of them have the jewels. We've asked them to wait for further questioning in the Jewel House."

"What about the other tourists on the grounds?" Jack asked.

"We've searched them, too, and found nothing. Because of that," Tommy said, "we've had to let them go. Believe me, this one's a head-scratcher, which is why we called the GPF. We need your help to solve the crime."

"Which one of the jewels was taken?" asked Jack, knowing that the Crown Jewels were made up of many crowns, orbs, and scepters.

"The Imperial State Crown, the Sovereign's Orb, *and* the Sovereign's Scepter with Cross," said Tommy.

"No way!" said Jack. Given the value and importance of what was stolen, he

knew this was going to be a special
case. The Sovereign's Scepter with Cross
contained the finest cut diamond in the
world, the Cullinan I.

"Why don't I take you over to the
Jewel House?" offered Tommy. "The six
people who were in there at the time of
the theft are being held there. Maybe you
can speak to them and get something
out of them. Frankly," he added, "I'm

not sure they had anything to do with this."

Tommy led Jack up Water Lane and past the Medieval Palace, St Thomas's Tower, and Traitors' Gate. They hung a left at the Wakefield Tower and walked under a stone archway. As they climbed another cobblestone street, Jack spied some black cages through a crumbling stone wall on his right.

"That's where the ravens are," said Jack, pointing in the direction of the gaps. He remembered seeing them on his last visit. "Is it true that if one of them leaves, it means that there will be no more kings and queens of England?"

"That's what they say, young man," said Tommy. "I'm not sure I entirely believe it. But, just in case, we clip their wings so that there's no chance of finding out."

Chapter 5:
The Interrogation

Tommy led Jack past a large building with four turrets. This was the White Tower— the oldest part of the Tower of London. It was built after William the Conqueror captured London in 1066. Jack climbed a few stairs to the top of the courtyard. To his left was a paved area with a monument in the middle.

"That's Tower Green," said Tommy, nodding in the direction of the monument. "That marks the place where seven famous people were beheaded."

"Like Anne Boleyn," said Jack, who'd remembered that Henry VIII had executed his second wife here.

"And Catherine Howard," added Tommy, naming another of Henry's wives. "Lord Hastings was beheaded here, too."

Jack gulped at the thought of what it would feel like to have your head chopped off by an ax. He and Tommy hurried past Tower Green and towards a large golden-colored building that was newer than the others.

"Here we are," said Tommy, pointing to the building. "This is Waterloo Barracks. Inside is the Jewel House." He motioned for Jack to follow him.

Beyond the doorway was a series of
rooms with giant movie screens, each
one playing a film about the history of
the Queen's jewels. Walking through, they
reached an open vault door that led to
where the Crown Jewels were kept.

In the middle of the room were five
glass cases standing in a row. Each one
was as tall as a man and was capped
with steel on the top and stone at the

bottom. On either side of the cases was a flat, moving walkway. A clever way, Jack reckoned, to keep the tourists moving through. Because of the theft, the walkway was now turned off.

Jack walked over and looked closely at the cases. The Imperial State Crown was missing from one, while the Sovereign's Scepter with Cross and the Sovereign's Orb were missing from others. The glass around the case wasn't broken and, as far

as Jack could tell, the top and bottom were still intact. The only thing left was the red and gold pillow on which the jewels once lay.

In the corner of the room were the six people who had been present at the time of the crime. There was a church vicar and a younger man, a mother and her daughter, and an elderly couple. The elderly woman was standing with the help of a walking stick.

Based on first impressions, Jack was going to have to agree with Tommy. They didn't look like a bunch of criminals. More importantly none of them looked as if they were carrying the Crown Jewels.

Jack opened his Book Bag and grabbed his Encryption Notebook. As soon as he placed his thumb over the glass, the Encryption Notebook turned itself on, read his thumbprint, and identified him as the rightful owner. Jack detached the pen from the side of the gadget and made a note of the date: May 9th.

When he was ready, he approached the vicar and the young man.

"Hi there," said Jack. "My name is Jack Stalwart." He turned to the vicar first. "Can I have your name?" he asked.

"Father Type," he answered, smiling.

Jack turned to the younger man. "And yours?" he asked.

"Edward Pigeon," he replied.

"Thanks," said Jack, making a few notes on their appearance. Father Type, in particular, had a familiar look about him.

"Would you mind stepping over here while I ask you a few more questions?" He wanted to make sure that they had some privacy and led the men over to a side room where the Queen's priceless coronation robe hung in a massive glass case.

"Where do you work?" Jack asked, carrying on with the interrogation.

"We both work just off of Tooley Street," said the vicar.

Jack thought about churches near Tooley Street in London. "At Southwark Cathedral?" he asked, remembering the location of that famous church.

"Yes, that's right," said Father Type, nodding. "At Southwark Cathedral."

"I was wondering," said Jack, turning to the vicar first, "if you could describe exactly what you saw."

"Nothing significant, my child," replied Father Type. "We were on the walkway

like everyone else," he explained, "adoring the Queen's precious jewels. All of a sudden, the lights went out and when they came back on, the jewels were gone. It gave me quite a fright, really," he added, shaking his head.

Jack turned to Edward Pigeon. "Did you see the same thing as Father Type?" he asked the young man.

"Yes," said Edward. "Pity really—I only saw the jewels for a few seconds before they vanished."

Jack thanked both men for their time and called the mother and daughter over. He introduced himself, took their details, and asked whether they had noticed anything important.

"Well," said the mother, "I do remember hearing something when the lights went out. It sounded as though someone was whispering something."

"Do you remember whether it was a man or a woman?" asked Jack.

"It was a man, I think," she answered, "although the voice was a bit high-pitched. So I suppose it could have been either."

"And what about you?" said Jack, turning to the young girl. "What do you remember?"

"Nothing," said the girl. She hid herself in her mother's skirt.

Thinking he'd got all he was going to

get out of these two, Jack called the
elderly couple over.

"Hi there," he said. He introduced
himself and noted down both their names
and their contact details. "Can you tell me

whether you saw or heard anything significant before the Crown Jewels went missing?'

"I didn't hear anything, but I certainly smelled something," said the man.

This was interesting, thought Jack. He made a note of it in his Notebook.

"What did it smell like?" he asked.

"Something sweet," said the woman. "Kind of like berries."

"Is there anything else you can remember?" asked Jack.

"Nothing," said the man. The woman agreed.

Jack looked at his Notebook and reviewed the information he'd gathered so far on his suspects:

Father Type and Edward Pigeon
(Southwark Cathedral, London)

Nancy and Polly Sommerville
(Brighton, East Sussex)

Ned and Phyllis Royale (Alton,
Hampshire)

He then made a note of the sequence
of events:

Tourists on walkway
Lights go out
Sound of whispering
Smell of something sweet

After securing what Jack thought was
enough information about the suspects,
he and Tommy let them leave the Tower
of London.

"What did I tell you, Jack?" said Tommy,
turning to him. "It's a head-scratcher,
isn't it?"

"Sure is," said Jack. There were no obvious suspects and no obvious means by which the jewels had been stolen.

Tommy looked at his watch, and then looked at Jack. "We need to find the crooks soon," he said. "With three hours left, we're running out of time."

Chapter 6:
The Scam

Jack looked at his Encryption Notebook again and reviewed his notes. *Smell of something sweet, probably ladies perfume. Sound of man or woman whispering in the dark.* He sniffed the air. He didn't smell anything sweet. He listened closely. He couldn't hear anything unusual.

He walked over to the cases again and looked inside. Jack could tell from the indentation in the pillow that the crown itself was fairly large. The scepter was long with a pointed end and the orb was big and round. Whoever took them would need to put them in something big.

Jack found Tommy, who was in the other room, chatting to another Beefeater. Tommy introduced the other man as Charles.

"Pleased to meet you, Charles," said

Jack. "I'm trying to narrow down all the different ways someone could have taken the jewels out of their cases," he explained. "Could someone have taken them from above?" Jack was thinking that perhaps the tops had been dismantled ahead of time and lifted off without anyone knowing it.

"Nope," said Charles. "Not possible. Every morning and night the case is checked from top to bottom to make sure it's intact. Besides," he added, "it's made of impenetrable steel. It would be almost impossible to cut through it anyway."

"What about from below?" asked Jack, who was running out of options. If it wasn't from the top or the sides, then it had to be from underneath.

"No chance there either," said Tommy. "Each jewel sits on a pillow which then sits on a stand. The stand is a moveable

platform that travels down to the Jewel
Master's quarters on the lower ground
level. Once there, the Jewel Master takes
off the jewel, cleans it and then places it
back on the pillow. He then returns it up
to the case.

"You see," he continued, "no one but
the Jewel Master has access to the jewels.
The only way to lower and raise that
platform is if you have an access code.
And only the Jewel Master knows it. And
before you think that he's had anything to

do with this, consider that he's nearly eighty years old and has worked here for over fifty-five years. Besides," he added, "he's on holiday with his daughter in Greece and the room is under surveillance. We've checked that camera, too."

"Well, if someone were going to steal the Crown Jewels, how would they do it?" asked Jack.

"You got me," said Charles. "It would take a miracle. The only time anyone's been able to pull off a stunt like this was on the ninth of May 1671. Colonel Blood was his name," he said, "and he did it by dressing up like a vicar. He brought along a pal named Thomas Parrot and the two of them made off with the jewels before being caught—" Charles stopped himself as soon as he realized what he'd said.

Jack was stunned. He couldn't believe his ears. He'd been fooled. They'd all been fooled! He looked through his Notebook once again. The name the vicar had given him was Father Type. Blood has different groups like Type A and Type B. His young assistant was Edward Pigeon— which was very similar to Thomas Parrot!

The two men were playing games with Jack from the start. He stamped his feet on the ground and growled in frustration. Father Type and Thomas Pigeon had pulled off the unimaginable. They had stolen the Crown Jewels and Jack, Tommy, and Charles had unknowingly let them escape.

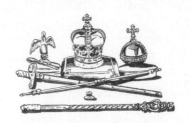

Chapter 7:
The Discovery

But who were these guys and where were the jewels? The men definitely didn't have them when they left.

Jack looked down at the Encryption Notebook. Father Type and Edward Pigeon had said they worked at Southwark Cathedral. Deciding that was as good a place to start as any, Jack pulled out his map of London. Southwark Cathedral wasn't far away.

Pressing the ENCRYPT button on his

Notebook, Jack said a quick goodbye to Tommy and Charles, making sure he had Tommy's contact details in case of an emergency. He hurried out of the Jewel House, past Traitors' Gate, down Water Lane, and under the spiky gate.

Once outside the Tower, he jumped on a massive red double-decker bus and found a seat on the upper deck. Jack figured the view from there was as good as any. As the bus lurched forward and began to move through the streets of London, he kept his eyes open for Father Type, Edward Pigeon, or any other clue that might help solve the crime.

The bus chugged across Tower Bridge and over to the other side of the River Thames, which was one of the biggest rivers in England. As they drove along Tooley Street, Jack could see Southwark Cathedral straight ahead. It was a

beautiful church with a small garden at
the front where visitors could stop and
have a drink or an ice cream. Jack hopped

off the bus and walked briskly towards it. He entered the church and looked around.

To his left was what Jack had been hoping for—a notice board. He walked over and scanned through the pictures of the clergy. Unfortunately—but unsurprisingly—there wasn't a picture of anyone resembling Father Type. He looked for one like Edward Pigeon. Nothing there either.

Jack exited the church and paused outside. He thought back to his conversation with the two men. Father Type had said that they worked "off Tooley Street" which Jack took to mean Southwark Cathedral. It was the closest church to that street that he could think of. A basic mistake, he thought. He had given the criminal an answer he could use; he should have let the man provide the information himself.

Although they obviously had nothing to

do with the church, maybe the two men really did work off Tooley Street. Making tracks, Jack left the church garden and headed for that road. Once on it, he could see a sign for one of London's most popular attractions, the London Dungeon.

He stopped and looked at the advertisement for the dungeon's latest exhibits: EXPERIENCE THE GREAT PLAGUE! WITNESS THE GREAT FIRE OF LONDON! Although it was an unlikely place to find these men, Jack bought a ticket and went inside. He quickly looked around and when he was satisfied there was no sign of them, left the dungeon and carried on.

Soon he saw a poster advertising a show at the Magic Theater. He remembered this place from when he came to see Ivan the Incredible with his Uncle Richard. He approached a poster listing all the performances.

49

Ivan the Incredible! The greatest illusionist of all time . . . Witness him escape from a fiery pit! Watch an elephant disappear before your very eyes! Book now, or miss out. Last show, tonight 5:00 PM.

In the lower right-hand corner of the poster was a picture of Ivan the Incredible and his assistant dressed in their costumes from the show. Jack leaned closer to have a look. Underneath the costumes, their wigs, and their beards, Jack noticed something familiar.

Now everything made sense. The lights going out, the sweet smell of berries, the chanting and the cleverly faked names— all these were tactics magicians used to distract their audiences. Yes, Jack thought, there was no doubt. Father Type was Ivan the Incredible and Edward Pigeon his loyal assistant, Jazz.

Chapter 8:
The Preparation

But why would Ivan and Jazz want to steal the Crown Jewels in the first place? Weren't they worried that someone like Jack would recognize them? Perhaps, Jack figured, for a showman like Ivan a crime wasn't worth committing if it wasn't done in front of an "audience."

Jack looked at his watch. It was 4:00 PM. He needed to think of a plan before Ivan the Incredible's last show started at 5:00 PM. Jack knew that if he didn't catch him tonight, the jewels would probably be lost for ever.

He ducked into a nearby café and ordered a smoothie. He pulled out his Encryption Notebook, set it back to normal, and made a list of what he remembered of Ivan's last show. He marked an "X" beside the trick where he planned to spring his trap. If everything went according to plan, Jack would have an easy time bringing this magic madman to justice.

Double-checking the contents of his Book Bag, he took a sip of his drink and looked at his Watch Phone. It was 4:30 PM. There was only half an hour to buy a ticket and get to his seat, ready for the show.

Jack hurried to the ticket office, bought a ticket near the stage, and went inside. By the time he'd found his seat, there were five minutes to go. The lights were starting to flicker—the show was about to begin.

A man's voice came over the loud speaker:

"Ladies and gentlemen, welcome to the Magic Theater. Tonight, you will be treated to a performance by one of the greatest magicians of all time—Ivan the Incredible! As tonight is his last performance, put your hands together to give him a warm welcome."

The audience around Jack erupted with wild applause.

Yes, thought Jack, I've got a very warm welcome for you indeed.

Chapter 9:
The Show

Almost as soon as the curtains opened, an incredible flash of light burst from the center of the stage and turned into a towering wall of flames. Jack was startled. He didn't remember this part of the show. He put his right hand over his eyes to shield them from the heat.

Carefully, he peeked through his fingers and spied Ivan the Incredible walking through the fire. Ivan emerged from the flames and stepped unharmed to the front of the stage towards his screaming fans. Although Ivan was a crook, Jack couldn't help but be impressed.

Ivan the Incredible lifted his arms to the audience, as if he were begging for applause. The dutiful spectators did just what he asked. They broke into such a roar of claps and cheers that Jack could barely think.

"Welcome! Welcome!" Ivan called to the audience. "So glad you could be here for my very last show! Tonight," he said, "is a very special night. It's special for two reasons. The first is that I have created a brand-new show just for you. Its theme is 'Kings and Queens,' in honor of this great country.

"The second," Ivan the Incredible continued, "is because an old friend of mine is sitting in the audience tonight." He looked down at Jack as a spotlight was directed on top of him. "His name is Jack

Stalwart, and if you give him some
encouragement, maybe he will join me on
stage later tonight."

The audience whistled and cheered for

Jack, who slumped down in his chair, trying not to be noticed.

How did he know I was here? he asked himself. Although Jack was sitting close to the stage, the lights had been out until Ivan had burst through the flames. This is terrible, thought Jack. Not only had Ivan changed the show, he'd ruined Jack's chances of making an arrest without causing a big fuss.

The crowd started chanting again: "Ivan . . . Ivan . . . Ivan . . ."

Ivan the Incredible looked at Jack and smiled before turning back towards the soaring flames. He walked through them again, but this time, as he did so, the fire vanished, taking Ivan with it. Jack sat bolt upright in his chair. He wondered whether Ivan had left the show for good.

Within seconds, a beautiful white bird

flew down from the rafters and onto the
stage. Jack took a deep breath and settled
back into this seat. This was one of Ivan's
tricks. He hadn't left the show yet.

Chapter 10:
The Lure

Almost as soon as the bird landed, it
became Ivan the Incredible again. But this
time, he was dressed like Henry VIII, who
was King of England in the early 1500s.

From the right side of the stage, Jack
could hear a noise. It sounded as if someone were pushing something heavy on
rollers.

"Ladies and gentlemen!" said Ivan.
"As promised, I have themed this show
around the great kings and queens of
Britain. For my first feat of illusion, I

would like to re-enact the beheading of Lord Hastings, ordered by Henry the Eighth. And I would like my kind friend, Jack Stalwart, to join me onstage."

Jack's eyes widened. A large round block of wood was being rolled onto the stage by Ivan's assistant, Jazz. It looked like a tree stump. Stuck in the middle was a shiny, sharp ax with its handle pointing straight up in the air. Jack sat frozen in his seat. He gulped and looked around. He could hear the audience starting to chant his name. "Jack . . . Jack . . . Jack . . ."

He looked up at Ivan the Incredible, who was smiling and motioning for Jack to come onstage.

Jack didn't know what to do. He knew that magic was all about illusion. He knew that Ivan the Incredible wouldn't or couldn't actually behead him onstage.

But then again, this wasn't an ordinary evening. Ivan was trying to get away with a terrible crime and Jack was the only person standing in his way.

"No thanks," Jack shouted to Ivan.

"Did you hear that, audience?" yelled
Ivan. "He's a bit nervous. Why don't we
give Jack some encouragement?" He lifted
his arms and waved his hands at the
throngs of men, women, and children in
the theater.

The audience's chants grew louder. They
were cheering for Jack. Above the noise,
he heard a man from two rows back.

"Come on, kid!" the man shouted. "It's
just a magic trick!" He's right, Jack told
himself, trying to
stay calm. It is just
a magic trick.
There was no
way Ivan could
hurt Jack in front
of all these
people. Besides,
getting onstage

might give Jack a chance to figure out where the Crown Jewels actually were.

"All right! All right!" said Jack as he grabbed his Book Bag and made his way onstage.

Chapter 11:
The Ax

"So wonderful to see you again," said Ivan to Jack as he placed his hand on Jack's back. Ivan led him towards Jazz, who was waiting next to the wooden block. The audience was chanting in the background.

"I know you took the jewels," said Jack, looking up at Ivan. "Why don't you just tell me where they are and we can forget about the whole thing?"

"I don't know what you're talking about," Ivan said, smiling. "I don't see any jewels around here." He shoved Jack towards Jazz and turned back to his adoring audience.

"Ladies and gentleman," said Ivan, assuming the role of Henry VIII. "The person before you is a traitor!" He turned around and pointed to Jack. "He has committed the crime of high treason and is therefore sentenced to death by beheading."

While Ivan was talking to his audience, Jazz pulled the ax out of the wood. He motioned for Jack to put his neck in place. Jack knelt down before the block, looking at the deep cut where the ax had been. There was no doubt something sharp had made that cut. He just hoped for his sake it wasn't this ax. Jack reluctantly lowered his head.

"Ladies and gentlemen!" said Ivan as Henry VIII. "The beheading of Lord Hastings!"

Quickly, Jack closed his eyes. In the background he could hear Jazz pick up the ax and swing it into the air before letting it come down over Jack's neck.

He was aware of a funny feeling on his neck and then felt something warm dripping over his ears.

Slowly, he opened his eyes and lifted his head. To his relief and amazement the rest of his body came with it. Jazz hadn't cut his head off after all and the warm feeling was just fake blood that had oozed out of the magic ax.

The theater was filled with applause. This time, the cheers weren't just for Ivan and Jazz. They were for Jack, too. As Jack started to move offstage, Jazz came up behind him.

"Leave us alone," he said, grabbing Jack's left arm tightly, "or we'll kill you for real."

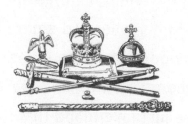

Chapter 12:
The Revelation

Tired from nearly having his head chopped off, Jack made his way off the stage and back to his seat. Ivan the Incredible left the stage briefly and came back dressed as a different king before he spoke to the audience.

"Now we are fast-forwarding our journey through the kings and queens of the past to Charles the Second. Charles the Second, as many of you will know, was king during the Great Plague of 1665 and the Great Fire of London in 1666. He also made two of the three Crown Jewels that the Queen uses today."

That fact made Jack's ears prick up. He wondered where Ivan was going with this "act" and whether there was going to be some sort of clue that would lead Jack to where the jewels were being kept. He listened carefully to what Ivan the Incredible had to say.

"King Charles the Second created this beautiful orb," said Ivan. At the mention of the orb, Ivan lifted his left hand. From nowhere, a bubble appeared above his hand with an image of the orb sitting in a glass case. Jack rubbed his eyes, as did the girl sitting next to him.

"He also created this beautiful scepter," added Ivan as he conjured another image into the air, this time of the scepter inside its glass case. "Sitting at the top of the scepter," he explained, "is the First Star of Africa, also known as the Cullinan I, the largest cut diamond in the world!

"Finally," he said, "the third and final treasure was not created by Charles the Second, but by George the Sixth in 1937."

POOF!

At the mention of this new king's name, Ivan's costume changed to that of George VI.

"The Imperial State Crown was made in 1937," continued Ivan. "Some say it's the most beautiful piece in the entire collection. There are over 2,800 diamonds and 270 pearls." With a wave of his hand, he created a third image in the air, one of

the Imperial State Crown, also in a glass
case.

Looking at the images, Jack had a
horrible idea. What if the jewels really
were still in their cases, just as Ivan was
showing them? Jack had been baffled by

how Ivan and Jazz had escaped with the jewels from the Tower; they were so big. But perhaps, Jack thought, they never did. Maybe the jewels were still in the Jewel House. Maybe Ivan and Jazz had created an illusion to make Jack and Tommy think the jewels had been stolen, so they could actually steal them another time.

"Yes, ladies and gentlemen," said Ivan, causing Jack to snap out of his thoughts, "this is our last glimpse into the world of the kings and queens. Our journey ends here with a lasting image for all of you of the jewels that we have stolen tonight." Ivan paused and then added, "We bid you farewell!" Then the two men disappeared in a puff of smoke before Jack had time to register what they had said.

Chapter 13:
The Mad Dash

Jack was stunned. Like the rest of the
audience, he was trying to work out
whether this was a trick or if what Ivan
had said was true. As the audience was
whispering, Jack hurried onto the stage.
Ducking in and out of the wings, he
looked for any sign of Ivan and Jazz. But
they had completely disappeared.

Jack returned to the spot where they
had been standing. Wondering if they'd
used a trap door, he looked down. Sure
enough, there was a small copper ring. He

bent down and pulled it hard. A thin rectangular door flew open. He lowered himself through the hole and climbed down a flight of narrow steps. As soon as he reached the lower level, he started running. In the distance he could hear Ivan and Jazz.

"Quick!" said one of the men.

"He's coming!" said the other.

BANG!

It sounded like a door. Jack ran as fast as he could, down a long hall and towards the sounds of the men. As he ran, he passed photos of Ivan and Jazz in various poses and outfits. When he reached a steel door, he flung it open.

BLAM!

In front of Jack was the Magic Theater car park. It was full to the brim of parked cars. So many, in fact, that it was an absolute jam. There's no way that Ivan and Jazz can get themselves out of this, thought Jack.

BBRRRMMM!

In the distance a motorcycle engine revved up. Jack looked in the direction of the noise and saw Ivan and Jazz speeding down the road on a red Ducati.

"Drat!" said Jack, frustrated they'd escaped by motorcycle. I have to warn Tommy, he said to himself as he dialed Tommy's number on his Watch Phone. But there was no answer.

Working quickly, Jack knelt down. He unzipped his Book Bag and pulled out a miniature disc. Placing his hands on the outside of the disc, he slid them around until the disc grew larger. He then grabbed a small steel rod and pulled it three times until it grew to be taller than he was.

Plunging the rod into a small hole at the edge of the disc, Jack pushed the button marked PROP on his Watch Phone. Instantly, two propellers shot out of the rod and began to spin. This was the GPF's Heli-Spacer—Jack's only hope for getting to the Tower on time.

He hopped on and clipped the Heli-Spacer's belt around himself. Then he

raised his hands in the air. The Heli-Spacer began to rise. All Jack needed was one good thrust. As he threw his arms forward, the Heli-Spacer took off. Soon Jack was flying over the River Thames in pursuit of Ivan and Jazz.

Chapter 14:
The Groans

Within minutes, Jack was hovering above Tower Green. He slowly dropped his hands to his sides and he was lowered safely to the ground. After touching down, he hopped off, took apart the device and packed it away.

Jack glanced at his Watch Phone. It was 6:30 PM.

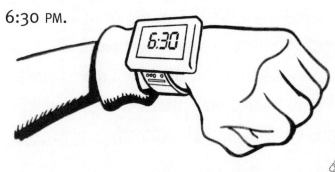

He dialed Tommy's number again, but still there was no answer. He looked across the courtyard and spied Ivan and Jazz. They were making their way to the entrance of the Jewel House. Keeping low, Jack ran towards the doors and pressed his ear against them to listen. There were no sounds from Ivan and Jazz. Quickly, he entered the first chamber.

As he moved from room to room, Jack was aware of two things: 1) There was no sign of Ivan and Jazz anywhere; and 2) Tommy and Charles were missing, too. None of the other Beefeaters seemed to be around either.

When he reached the last room, Jack was relieved. Sitting on top of their red and gold pillows were the "missing" crown, scepter and orb. The Crown Jewels hadn't been stolen after all. They were tucked away in their protective cases. The

illusion that Ivan and Jazz had created
had stopped working.

Then, out of nowhere, Jack heard something strange. It sounded like someone or something groaning. He pulled his Ear Amp out of his pocket and hooked it into the inside of his ear. Although it resembled a tiny kidney bean, the Ear Amp could make even the faintest of sounds seem much louder.

As he listened, Jack could hear the noise more clearly. It was human and it was coming from the floor above. Unfortunately for Jack, there was no obvious way up to the upper level. The only way he could get to the next floor was to slice through the ceiling. He looked a bit closer—it was made of stone.

Figuring the Queen wouldn't mind a little inconvenience like a hole in the ceiling, Jack clambered on top of the orb's case and pulled out his Rock Corer.

The Rock Corer worked a bit like an apple corer, but it could slice a tunnel through hard rock.

Jack set the width to the size of his own body. Strapping on some goggles to protect his eyes, he pulled the cord. Sounding like an electric saw, the Rock Corer began to eat away the stone. Within minutes, Jack had created a hole big enough to crawl through. He put the gadget away and heaved himself up to the next level. In the corner, he could see Tommy and four other Beefeaters. He raced over to them and crouched down.

"Are you all right?" Jack asked.

"Uhhhh," groaned Tommy. He tried to focus his eyes and look at Jack. "It was the vicar," he explained. "He came back after you left. He said something to us," he added. "I don't remember anything after that."

"He hypnotized you," explained Jack. "And put you in a trance."

"Huh?" said Tommy.

"He's not a vicar," said Jack. "He's a magician. And he's in the building right now! He's come to steal the Crown Jewels."

"What?" said Tommy, sounding confused. "What do you mean? They've already been stolen."

"Not quite," said Jack. "I'll explain later. Are there any secret passages in the barracks?" He wasn't sure how they would have known about them, but he was guessing that Ivan and Jazz had used them to leave the building.

"Yeah," said Tommy. "In the first room as you enter the Jewel House there are several wooden panels. Behind the panel with 'Elizabeth the Second' on it is a door that leads you downstairs to the Jewel Master's Quarters."

"Perfect," said Jack. "I need to run. Are you going to be OK?" he asked Tommy.

"Of course," said Tommy. "Now go and catch those thieves."

Chapter 15:
The Getaway

Jack left Tommy and carefully lowered himself down on top of the glass case. He sat for a moment, thinking about the jewels in their cases. The only way Ivan and Jazz were going to be able to get to them was from the Jewel Master's Quarters underneath. Jack could use the Rock Corer to get to the lower level, or he could try to head them off at the front door.

WOOMPH!

Jack was startled by a noise. In fact, it wasn't just the sound. The case he was sitting on was starting to shake.

WOOMPH!

It happened again.

Quickly, Jack climbed off the case and onto the ground. Before his eyes, the scepter and the orb were being lowered down until they had vanished from sight.

WOOMPH!

The sound was coming from the other end of the room now. It was the case with the Imperial State Crown. It was being lowered down, too.

"Arrgh!" growled Jack in frustration. Ivan and Jazz were stealing the jewels! There was no time to try to use the secret passage. Jack's only option was to stop them as they left by the front door.

He dashed through the final chamber and towards the first room. Almost as soon as he entered the room with the panels, Ivan and Jazz burst out of the secret passage, crashing into him and sending him backwards onto the floor.

"Better luck next time, kid!" screamed Ivan as he and Jazz raced outside through the arched doorway. Both men were carrying bags on their backs. Sticking out of one of them was the top of the Scepter with Cross.

Jack had only seconds to recover. His back was hurting, but he didn't have time to think. Ivan and Jazz were getting away and Jack needed to stop them before they

committed a serious crime against the Queen.

Jack pulled himself together and ran after the thieves. Ivan and Jazz were sprinting across the courtyard to the left of the White Tower and under an archway. On the other side of the archway was the River Thames. Jack figured that Ivan and Jazz had a speedboat waiting so that they could make their escape.

Even though he was running as fast as he could, Jack was struggling to catch up with the crooks. Ivan and Jazz were bigger and their legs were twice as long. They'd already made it past the archway and were kneeling down next to the wall of the Thames. The only thing that could stop them was the GPF's Tornado. Smiling to himself, Jack pulled it out of his Book Bag and prepared to strike.

Chapter 16:
The Tornado

As Ivan and Jazz assembled their gear, Jack knelt down on the ground. He lifted the Tornado and set the switch to 2.

"Ready . . . Aim . . ." said Jack, and he pulled the launcher.

Two ropes shot out of the gadget towards Ivan and Jazz. As soon as they hit their targets, the ropes swirled furiously, again and again. They bound the crooks' feet first and then their hands.

"Noooo!" said Ivan, struggling to break out of its grip.

"Arrghhh!" yelled Jazz as he tried to bite off the rope.

But the power of the Tornado was too strong. Jack watched as the rope continued to wrap Ivan and Jazz up, so that in the end all you could see were their noses and mouths through two tiny windows.

When Jack reached the men, he had to laugh. Ivan and Jazz were so tightly wound that they looked like a pair of sausages.

"Let us go, you brat!" yelled Ivan. Jack could tell it was him by the look in his eyes.

"Sorry, guys," replied Jack, pleased that he'd foiled one of the greatest magicians of all time. "I'm afraid you've done this to yourselves. Let's just hope the Queen doesn't decide to chop your heads off."

As Ivan and Jazz cursed and tried to wriggle free, Jack called Scotland Yard. He figured Tommy wouldn't mind him calling them now. The caper of the Crown Jewels had been solved. Within minutes, the officers arrived and dragged Ivan and Jazz

away—since they couldn't walk. Jack reckoned they were probably going away for a very long time, if the Queen had anything to say about it.

Chapter 17:
The Surprise Visitor

As Jack stood there in the Tower grounds, reflecting on his mission, a friendly voice came from behind.

"Well done, son." It was Tommy. He was obviously feeling better. "I don't know how we can thank you enough," he said, putting out his hand to shake Jack's.

"It was nothing," said Jack. "It's my job."

Just then, he saw two black limousines driving smoothly but quickly through the Tower grounds.

"Uh-oh," said Tommy. "Looks like we've got company."

Jack watched as Secret Service agents hopped out of the car. They looked around before opening the back passenger door. Somebody important must be inside, Jack thought.

An older woman stepped out of the car. Jack couldn't believe his eyes. It was the Queen of England—Queen Elizabeth II— and she was walking straight towards him.

"So," she said, with a pleasant smile, "you must be Jack."

Jack stared with his mouth open. Tommy bowed to Her Majesty and Jack quickly did the same.

"I cannot thank you enough," said the Queen. "You have saved my most precious jewels. You are a very brave boy."

Jack figured Scotland Yard had contacted her with the news. "It was nothing, Your Majesty," he said, shrugging his shoulders.

She looked knowingly at Tommy and smiled. "If there's anything I can do for you, please do let me know."

Jack couldn't think of anything he could ask the Queen for, but then he remembered something. "Well," he said, "I kind of need some help with my homework."

"What kind of homework?" the Queen asked.

"I need to memorize all the kings and queens of England by tomorrow," said Jack.

"Let's see what we can do about that," said the Queen. "I know a bit about the subject," she added, smiling again. "Why don't you come with me and we'll give you a lift."

Jack turned to Tommy and waved

goodbye. Tommy did the same and added a wink.

Climbing into the limousine's backseat, Jack sat down opposite the Queen. She began to tell him about the British monarchy. Over the next hour, she taught him everything he needed to know, so that by the time the limousine arrived at his house there was no need to do any more homework.

"Thanks a lot," said Jack as he stepped out of the car.

"No," said the Queen, "thank *you*. I am extremely grateful for all that you've done."

"Don't mention it, Your Majesty," Jack replied, and he bowed politely.

The door to the limousine closed and the car pulled away, leaving Jack alone at the front gate to his house. Looking at his Watch Phone, Jack cringed. It was getting late; it was 9:00 PM.

Even though he figured his parents were asleep, there was no way he wanted to risk entering the house through the front door. If he got caught, he'd have to explain to his mother why he was out so late. After punching a few buttons on his Watch Phone, Jack was transported back to his room. As soon as he arrived, he looked at the clock on his bedside table. It was just after half-past seven.

He took off his Book Bag and hid it

under his bed. Changing into his pajamas, he brushed his teeth and crawled under the covers. Reaching into his bedside table, he pulled out *Master the Art of Magic*. Although he didn't like Ivan the Incredible anymore, Jack still loved magic.

"Now," he said as he turned to page thirty-two, "let's find another trick . . ."

Find out more about
Secret Agent Jack Stalwart at

www.jackstalwart.com

Great games, puzzles,
free downloads,
activities, competitions
and much more!

SECRET-AGENT NOTES

SECRET-AGENT NOTES

SECRET-AGENT NOTES

SECRET-AGENT NOTES

SECRET-AGENT NOTES

SECRET-AGENT NOTES

SECRET-AGENT NOTES

SECRET-AGENT NOTES

SECRET-AGENT NOTES

SECRET-AGENT NOTES

SECRET-AGENT NOTES

SECRET-AGENT NOTES

SECRET-AGENT NOTES

SECRET-AGENT NOTES

SECRET-AGENT NOTES

SECRET-AGENT NOTES

SECRET-AGENT NOTES

SECRET-AGENT NOTES

About the Author

Elizabeth Singer Hunt is originally from Louisiana, and now lives in California. Inspired by her love of travel, she created the Jack Stalwart series for her children.